Scaredy Bat

SERIES COLLECTION: BOOKS 4-6

Scaredy Bat and the Haunted Movie Set

Scaredy Bat and the Mega Park Mystery

Scaredy Bat and the Art Thief

By Marina J. Bowman

Illustrated by Paula Vrinceanu

CODE PINEAPPLE

First paperback edition October 2022

Written by Marina J. Bowman
Illustrated by Paula Vrinceanu
Book Design by Emy Farella

ISBN 978-1-950341-84-9 (paperback black & white)
ISBN 978-1-950341-85-6 (paperback color)
ISBN 978-1-950341-86-3 (ebook)

Published by Code Pineapple
www.codepineapple.com

For all who fear being in the spotlight, but step up anyway to share something important-ant with the world.

Also by Marina J. Bowman

SCAREDY BAT

A supernatural detective series for kids with courage, teamwork, and problem solving. If you like solving mysteries and overcoming fears, you'll love this enchanting tale!

#1 Scaredy Bat and the Frozen Vampires
#2 Scaredy Bat and the Sunscreen Snatcher
#3 Scaredy Bat and the Missing Jellyfish
#4 Scaredy Bat and the Haunted Movie Set
#5 Scaredy Bat and the Mega Park Mystery
#6 Scaredy Bat and the Art Thief

THE LEGEND OF PINEAPPLE COVE

A fantasy-adventure series for kids with bravery, kindness, and friendship. If you like reimagined mythology and animal sidekicks, you'll love this legendary story!

#1 Poseidon's Storm Blaster
#2 A Mermaid's Promise
#3 King of the Sea
#4 Protector's Pledge

Detective Team

Jessica
"the courage"

Ellie
aka Scaredy Bat
"the detective"

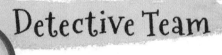

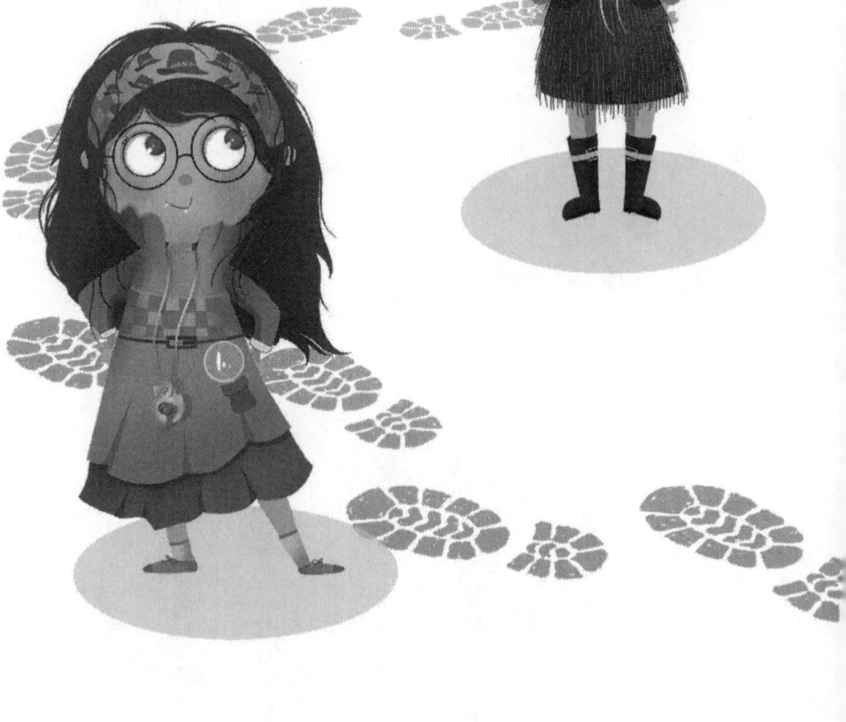

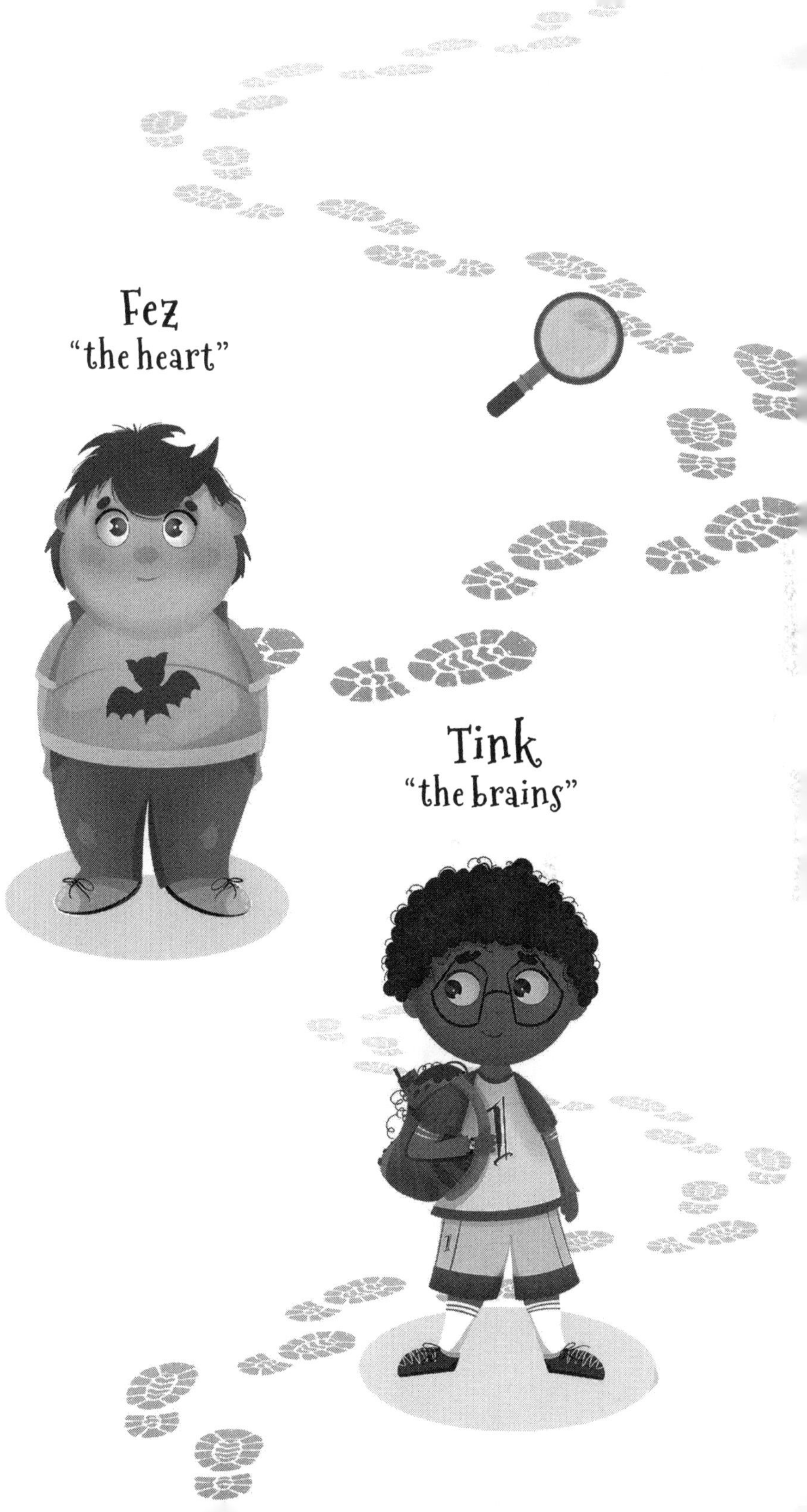
Fez
"the heart"
Tink
"the brains"

Scaredy Bat
and the Haunted Movie Set

By Marina J. Bowman

Illustrated by Paula Vrinceanu

CODE PINEAPPLE

Contents

Batty Bonuses

Can you solve the mystery?

All you need is an eye for detail, a sharp memory, and good logical skills. Join Ellie on her mystery-solving adventure by making a suspect list and figuring out who committed the crime! To help with your sleuthing, you'll find a suspect list template and hidden details observation sheets at the back of the book.

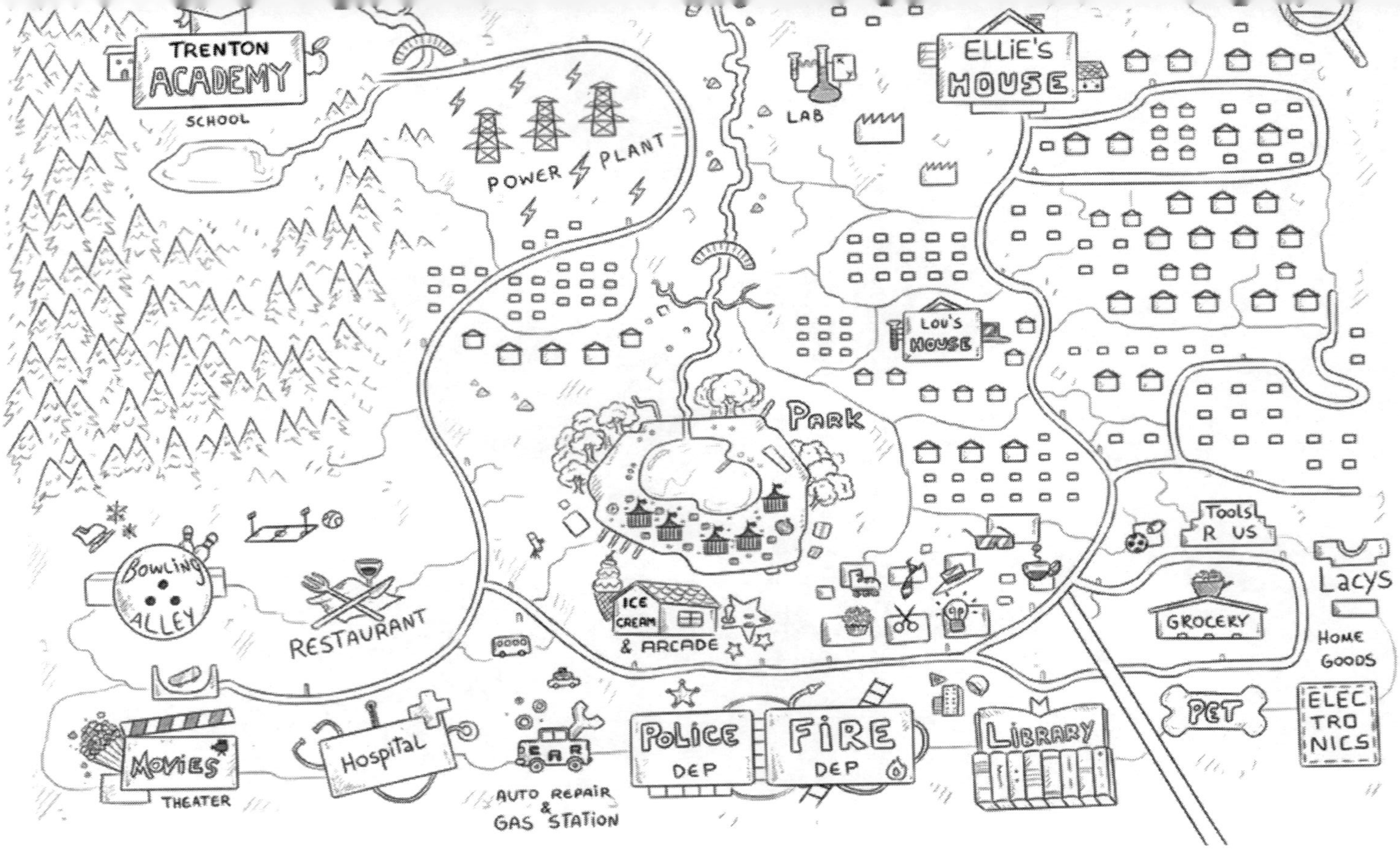
TRENTON ACADEMY
SCHOOL
POWER PLANT
LAB
ELLIE's HOUSE
LOU'S HOUSE
Park
BOWLING ALLEY
RESTAURANT
ICE CREAM & ARCADE
Tools R US
Lacys
HOME GOODS
GROCERY
MOVIES
THEATER
Hospital
CAR
AUTO REPAIR & GAS STATION
POLICE DEP
FIRE DEP
LIBRARY
PET
ELEC TRO NICS

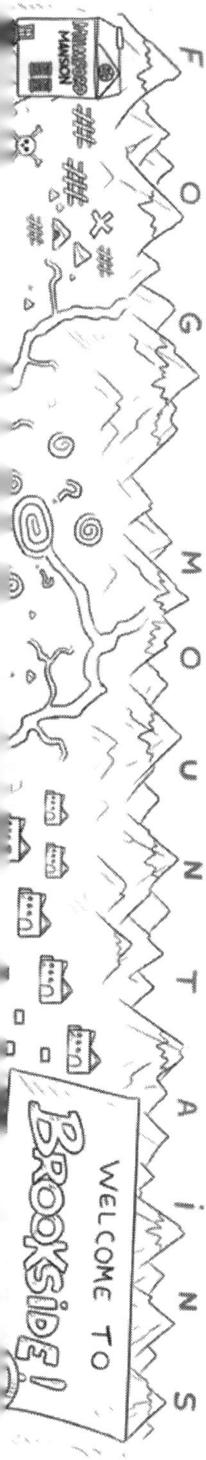

There's a place not far from here
With strange things 'round each corner
It's a town where vampires walk the streets
And unlikely friendships bloom

When there's a mystery to solve
Ellie Spark is the vampire to call
Unless she's scared away like a cat
Poof! There goes that Scaredy Bat

Villains and pesky sisters beware
No spider, clown, or loud noise
Will stop Ellie and her team
From solving crime, one fear at a time

Chapter One

Stuck in the Spotlight

"Ouch!" Ellie cried. A tentacle from her jellyfish costume was tangled in her long, brown hair—for the third time. "Jessica, I'm stuck again!" she called to her best friend across the dark, dusty dressing room. No one answered. The battered wood floor creaked as Ellie turned toward the pitter-patter of a sewing machine. She pushed aside a rusted metal rack of moth-eaten clothes. The rack's wheels screeched like hungry birds.

Jessica sat at a rickety dressing table in the corner. Above her hung a large painting of a groundhog wearing a dress. And beside her stood a bent floor lamp—the only light in the room. She twisted and turned a small piece of bright pink rubber underneath the machine's sewing needle. Every time she pressed the machine's pedal down, the lamp flickered.

"Jessica, I'm stuck," Ellie repeated. She was starting to sweat in the pink dress, which had strips of wispy fabric sewn all around it. She wished more than anything that the old dressing room's window wasn't boarded up so that she could open it. Or that there was air conditioning. Or that it would start snowing. Anything so she didn't feel like a hotdog sizzling on a fiery grill.

"Hold on," Jessica answered. "I'm working on something so you stop getting stuck." She looked at her watch. "We only have five minutes before showtime."

Ellie's heart pounded in her chest like a drum. She hated being in front of big crowds, especially on a stage. But when Jessica wanted to do a short play for their Jellyfish Lake presentation, she couldn't say no. Jessica was so excited about designing the costumes and set props. Plus, they were now one step closer to winning the prize for the best project—two tickets to the new amusement park, Mega Adventure Land. Too bad that also meant they had to perform in front of both grade 7 classes in five minutes. And then again for Parents' Night the next day.

"Tink and Fez just had to go flood the school gym with their jellyfish mucus project," Ellie said, fumbling with the tangle. "Now I have to perform in some spooky old theatre. This place probably hasn't been used since before we were born."

"Hey, we can hear you!" said Tink from the next room. "And Fez was the one who left the hose on in the gym."

"Am not!" Fez cried.

Ellie pulled at her tentacle tangle and let out a frustrated scream. "I need a mirror." Her tentacles dragged on the floor behind her as she stomped over to the next room. It was just as dusty and stuffy as the room she'd left, but this one didn't have a weird animal painting above the broken dressing table—it had a mirror. She tugged at the tangle, but it was hard to see that far behind her head. It didn't help that her hands kept shaking.

"Need some help?" a short boy with glasses and curly brown hair asked from the corner of the room. Ellie turned to see him standing beside a fish tank full of fake jellyfish.

"Yes, please," she said before noticing a pair of shiny scissors in Tink's hand. "But not with scissors!"

Tink looked down at the silvery shears and laughed. "No scissors. We were just putting some final touches on our presentation. Fez thought it needed more cardboard jellyfish. And less water." He placed the scissors on an armchair in the corner and started on the tangle. "Hey, why do you have a reflection?" he asked. "I thought vampires weren't supposed to."

"Ooo, that's a good question! Wait, don't answer yet," said Fez. A metal bowl crashed to the ground with a clatter as the boy with round cheeks and a big smile ran across the room. He wiped his hands on his jeans. They left behind a streak of fake jellyfish mucus. Or, as Fez liked to call it, jellyfish snot. "Ick. This fake jellyfish snot is so slippery and slimy," he said. He wiped his hands once more. "Okay, now answer!"

Ellie giggled. Her two human friends were always so curious about vampire life.

"That's just an old rumor," she answered. "They used to think vampires weren't living, so we couldn't have reflections. But if that were true, why would a chair have a reflection?" She pointed to the chair with the scissors. "It isn't living. Neither are those scissors."

Their teacher, Mr. Bramble, poked his head in the room. "Miss Spark, you and Miss Perry are up next."

Ellie took a deep, shaky breath. "I don't think I can do this," she said.

"You know, you already did the presentation once, and it was fine," Tink said. Ellie's hair was finally free from the tentacle's grip.

"That's not the same!" Ellie protested. "That was just in the classroom in front of Mr. Bramble."

"Okay, why don't you just imagine the whole audience as Mr. Bramble?" Tink said.

"Or you can imagine the audience in their underwear!" said Fez. "I hear that works for stage fright."

Ellie stuck out her tongue and squeezed her eyes shut. "Yuck! No, no, no. Now I'm just thinking of a hundred Mr. Brambles in their undies!" They all laughed. Jessica's red curls bounced as she ran into the bathroom with her newest creation.

"This will solve your tangle problem!" she said. She stretched a pink rubber swimming cap on Ellie's head and tucked her hair under it. The cap had an umbrella on the top with more tentacles glued around it that flowed to the floor.

Ellie wrinkled her nose. "I smell like a rubber duck. Are you sure this will be better?"

"Only one way to find out!" Jessica said. She put on her sunglasses and straw hat for the play. "Come on!" She grabbed Ellie's hand and took off running. Ellie's tentacles flew behind them like kite strings until they stopped behind the red velvet curtain.

"Ready?" Mr. Bramble asked, holding the curtain cord.

Jessica nodded and gave Ellie's hand a squeeze. "You've got this!"

"Good luck!" said another finalist. Ava Grinko gave Ellie a thumbs-up and smiled a big, fangy grin. Her black ringlets and button nose were the last things Ellie saw before the curtains rolled up. On the other side was a large room packed with fifty students sitting in rows of chairs. The crystal chandelier hanging in the middle of the room dimmed, making the birds painted on the ceiling fade to black. A spotlight shone on Jessica as she took a few steps forward.

"I am so excited to visit Jellyfish Lake," she said, pretending to walk by a lake. "I can't wait to see all the jellyfish." She looked around the lake. "Oh, there is one! But where are all of its friends?" The spotlight floated over to Ellie. She stood frozen in the hot light. The only part of her moving was her shaking hands, which made some of the tentacles on her costume vibrate. "Hello, jellyfish, where are all your friends?" Jessica asked.

Ellie went to open her mouth, but only a small squeak came out. All eyes were on her. She nervously thumbed the purple dragon pendant around her neck.

"Are your friends missing?" Jessica asked after a few moments of silence. Ellie nodded, her face as white as a cloud.

"My—my friends got stu-stuck," Ellie stuttered. She took a step forward. *RIP!* A tentacle tore off her dress. As she looked down, the tentacles from her hat covered her eyes.

She pushed them aside and cleared her throat. "My jellyfish friends— Woah!" Ellie tripped on another tentacle and fell to the ground with a *THUMP*. Her eyes filled with tears as the whole room broke into laughter.

Chapter Two

Worst Day Ever

Ellie bolted backstage and threw her jellyfish hat on the ground. The heavy curtains closed behind her, but the laughter still echoed through. She couldn't believe she'd tripped in front of everyone on stage. Tears streamed down her face as she tugged at the hot, rubbery jellyfish costume. The flurry of tentacles wrapped around her shaky hands, making it impossible to reach the back zipper.

"Are you okay?" Fez asked, rushing to Ellie with Tink by his side.

"No!" Ellie cried. She sobbed harder as she tugged on the costume. Her heart was hammering so hard it felt like it was going to burst through her chest.

"It's okay," Tink said. "Everyone makes mistakes."

"The only mistake I made was agreeing to this play!" Ellie sobbed. She gasped for air as she frantically tugged at the jellyfish costume. As she pulled, her elbow smacked a bottle on a table.

SMASH! The glass bottle shattered on the floorboards. The air flooded with the strong smell of sweet and flowery perfume. Ellie started coughing, making it even harder to breath.

"I can't breathe," Ellie said as she gasped for air.

"I think you're having a panic attack," Tink said. "Slow down your breathing." The two boys stood there with wide eyes, unsure of how to help. Ellie's top snapped back to her skin like a rubber band as she tried to tug it off. She felt something loosen around her neck, but the costume still gripped her.

"Get this costume off of me!" she cried.

Fez stepped toward Ellie, but Jessica got there first.

"It's okay," Jessica said. "Just breathe. I'll get you out." In one swift tug, Jessica got the zipper down, and Ellie scrambled out of the costume. She stood beside the shards of broken glass in a tank top and shorts. She bent over and planted her hands on her knees, her breathing still fast and loud.

"Are you okay?" Fez asked once again. Ellie was silent for a moment. Soon her breathing slowed, and she stood up straight. She wiped the tears and sweat streaming down her face with her hands.

"I think so," Ellie said. "But I am never, ever, EVER getting on stage again!" Ellie looked at the pink costume puddled on the floor. "And I am never wearing that costume again."

"But we have to perform for Parents' Night!" Jessica protested. "If we don't, we have no chance of winning those tickets to Mega Adventure Land."

"I don't care," Ellie said. "No tickets are worth being embarrassed again."

Jessica lowered her voice. "I also have

someone coming to see the costumes. I wasn't going to tell you unless I got picked, but a theatre company is giving internships for winter break. I might get one if they like the play's costumes!"

Ellie was too upset to respond. Even though she thought that was really cool.

"After my dress wasn't picked as a finalist for the Hailey Haddie movie, I was really bummed and mad," Jessica added. "Especially after I found out Ava's dress made the finals. I wanted to give up on designing clothes. But instead, I worked really hard on this project. I think it's my best work."

"We worked really hard on our project too!" Ava said as she entered the backstage area. She stopped and stared at the broken perfume bottle scattered across the floor.

"You ruined my project," Ava said in a sad whisper, her bright blue eyes glossy with tears. "Lily and I worked *so* hard on that. And we only collected enough Jellyfish Lake flowers to make two bottles. But I already gave the other away. If this is because my dress was picked for the contest and yours wasn't, then you're just a big—"

"I'm so sorry!" Ellie said. "I was trying to get this silly costume off, and I bumped it. It was a total accident."

"My costume is not silly!" Jessica shouted.

A cackling laugh echoed from behind the group. Jack Grinko gave a mischievous grin as he pushed his black bangs out of his eyes. They were a bright, piercing blue color, just like his sister Ava's.

"Big surprise that Scaredy Bat messes up again!" he taunted. "Turns out you're not a good actress OR detective." Ellie's hands balled into fists. The only thing that could make this day worse was Jack Grinko, a boy who delighted in teasing her and her friends.

"Just ignore him," Fez whispered. "He's not worth fighting with." Ellie knew Fez was right, but it took everything she had not to say something mean back. She knew she couldn't keep quiet, so she turned around and walked away. Tink, Fez, and Jessica followed.

"Aw, are Scaredy Bat and her little friends

running away!" Jack called after them.

"This is the worst day ever," Ellie said once back in the dressing room.

"I know what will cheer you up," Jessica said. "They're unpacking the Hailey Haddie movie set in the mansion out front. We won't be able to use our set passes until tomorrow, but we might still see Hailey Haddie. She's coming sometime today. My mom knows the director, and they're supposed to be shooting the first scene with her tonight at the moon eclipse."

The thought of seeing her hero made Ellie feel a bit better. Hailey Haddie played a vampire detective in movies. She was the reason Ellie wanted to be a detective.

After signing out with Mr. Bramble, the four friends headed to the mansion out front. Thoughts of the failed jellyfish play melted away as they hiked the steps to the mansion. The path snaked around giant statues of a chipmunk, fox, rat, and groundhog.

"Aw, these are so cute!" Fez exclaimed. "They even have one of Jessica." He pointed to the statue of the rat in the cowboy hat.

"I do not look like this rat when I transform!" Jessica said. "The animal I turn into when I sneeze is way cuter. And I don't have some weird hat."

Ellie giggled. She thought the statues all looked kind of creepy. She stared at the chipmunk with an eye patch and pirate hat that was as tall as she was. She couldn't decide if it was creepier than a groundhog in a dress. But it definitely beat the fox with a monocle and top hat.

"Like I need something else to be afraid of," Ellie mumbled. A chilly fog had settled on the mountain, making the large house they were headed toward look like a blur.

"How much money do you think you need to own a mansion with a theatre in the backyard?" Tink asked.

"A lot!" Jessica replied. "I read that Mr. Mumford was the richest man in the world when he was alive. Which makes sense. Who else builds their own personal theatre in their yard? He built it so vampire actors would have a place to perform when they were banned from all the other theatres. And some pretty awesome people have performed here. Like Leta Thomas, the first vampire actress ever to appear in a movie. And Theodore Mento, the most dreamy ghost ever."

As Jessica listed all the people who had performed at the Mumford Theatre, they reached the two-story brick mansion. Like the theatre, the brick was green in many spots with moss and long vines. Windows were missing shutters, and much of the glass was smashed, with some windows boarded up.

"Woah, this place is falling apart," Fez said.

Tink nodded. "That's why they picked it for the movie. They won't need a lot of set decorations to make it creepy." Ellie's gaze trailed toward the steep black roof with peeling shingles. A chimney poked out the top with a large, twiggy bird nest sitting on the edge. Ellie watched as a fat gray-and-black cat with a striped tail ran across the slope.

Suddenly, a short and stout woman burst through the mansion's front door. Her bright

blue eyes were thick with sparkly eye shadow, and her lips were painted with pink lipstick.

"I quit!" she yelled. "I will not work on a haunted movie set!"

Ellie gulped. "Haunted?"

Chapter Three
Super Haunted

"This house is haunted?" Ellie said, standing in front of the old mansion. She turned to Jessica and planted her hands on her hips. "You told me that was just a rumor!"

Jessica raised her hands in surrender. "As far as I know it is."

Ellie ran after the woman with heavy makeup, who was headed to a small green car. "Excuse me, did you say this place is haunted?"

"Yup, super haunted," the woman said as she popped open the car's trunk, which was filled with clothes. She threw her silver makeup case inside. "Strange things have been happening all day. Cameras stopped working;

items went missing. Some of my makeup was replaced by some weird, super sticky, purple goop. I almost glued a woman's lips together with what I thought was purple lip gloss! Good thing I noticed before I used it on her. It isn't worth working with that crazy director for this." The woman plunked down into the driver's seat and looked at Ellie for the first time. She scanned her turquoise detective coat and set pass.

At the same time, Ellie took in the woman's long gray hair, which trailed over the side of the set badge hanging around her neck. On it was the name *Marilyn Grin*. And underneath was her title, *Makeup Art.* Ellie caught a whiff of something familiarly sweet on the woman.

"If I were you, I would get out of here with your little friends," Marilyn said. Before Ellie could ask more questions, the engine started with a roar, the door slammed, and the little green car rolled away. Ellie turned toward her friends standing close behind her.

"Do you know what this means?" Ellie asked.

Fez nodded. "That this place might be haunted after all, and Jessica was wrong."

"Hey!" Jessica shouted, squinting at Fez.

Ellie giggled. "Maybe Jessica is wrong. But it means we have another mystery!" Ellie's stomach bubbled with excitement. She reached into her pocket and flipped open her detective notepad to scribble a few notes.

Clues

1. *Mysterious purple goop.*

Suspects

1. *Some sort of ghost – Wants people out of the house?*
2. *Marilyn Grin (makeup art) – Called director "crazy." Maybe wants some sort of revenge?*

Ellie thought it wasn't much, but Hailey Haddie's new book said a good detective needed to pay attention to all the details.

"If this is a mystery, we need to get inside and search for clues," Tink said.

"But how?" Jessica asked. "You can't get past security without set passes."

Ellie turned to the front door. "Let's just act normal, and maybe we can sneak in."

The house's floor creaked and groaned with every step they took in the narrow entryway. A bearded security guard sat on a stool near the door. He read a newspaper with a clown parade on the front and didn't bother to look up.

"Set badges, please," he said in a gruff voice, holding out a hand. Ellie's heart pounded harder.

"We, um, forgot them," said Jessica.

"Then come back when you have them," he said.

"Can't we just pop in really quick?" Tink asked.

"Nope," said the man, still looking at his newspaper.

"Wait," Ellie said, "We do have our passes." With a shaky hand, she unzipped the front pocket of Tink's backpack. She pulled out her set pass for the next day and covered the date with her thumb. Everyone else followed with the other passes. Ellie's anxiety swelled in her chest like a balloon. The man gave the passes a quick glance and stared at the group. After what felt like forever, he pointed to a sign-in sheet hanging on the wall.

"Sign in, and you're good to go," he said.

"You know, you guys have backpacks that you can store stuff in too," Tink said as he signed the sheet.

Ellie giggled. "But that's not as much fun." She was the last to sign her name. Once done, she stepped backward, right onto someone's foot.

"Ouch!" squeaked a man with a thick mustache and hat waiting behind her.

"I'm so sorry!" Ellie said. The man mumbled and quickly pushed past her to sign in.

"Come on!" Fez called from the end of the hall. "You have to see this!"

"Sorry again," Ellie said before racing to the end of the hall. The narrow entryway blossomed into a ginormous room with peeling wallpaper and high ceilings.

"Woah!" Ellie exclaimed. "I could probably

fit twenty of my bedrooms in here." She looked up at the clusters of cobwebs that suspended stout spiders between the wooden ceiling beams. Farther back in the room, a ladder stretched to a loft area lined with a worn wood railing. A sign sat near the top of the ladder: *Do Not Enter.*

Ellie made her way to a brown flowery sofa in the middle of the room. She ran her hand over the velvety fabric, which smelled like a damp basement. The sofa faced two ragged armchairs. Cameras and bright lights were set up around the furniture. Ellie's eyes turned into small slits as she took in the blinding lights, but Fez's did the opposite.

Fez's eyes grew wide as he spotted a far wall with a long table. On it was a tower of sprinkle cupcakes, a rainbow of cut fruit and vegetables, and a hot cheese fountain oozing with orange cheddar.

"I'm going to go search for clues over there!" Fez exclaimed. "I'll get you and Jessica some red velvet cupcakes, bell peppers, and cherries. I know how much you vampires love your

red food!"

Ellie smiled. He wasn't wrong. All vampires loved red food. The theory was they liked it so much because it reminded them of when they used to drink blood. Ellie was glad that wasn't a thing anymore. Well, except blood pudding. That was her favorite!

Tink licked his lips as he stared at the food. "We should work in pairs. I'll go with Fez."

Both girls laughed. Soon, a slurping sound came from behind them. A young woman with red hair and freckles dusting her narrow face was sucking down a drink with a straw. Ellie wrote down what the girl's badge said.

Misha May, Assistant

"Excuse me, Misha," Ellie said. "Do you mind if I ask you a few questions?"

"Look, kid," Misha said. "I am very busy." She crouched down to rummage in a backpack on the floor as she hummed a happy tune. Pinned to the front of the bag were buttons shaped like cats, cows, and other animals. It also had some stickers with words like *Ohio Girl*, *Misha*, and *Dream Big*.

"I just want to ask you if you've seen anything weird today," Ellie said.

"Fine, hold this," Misha said, pushing her cup into Ellie's hands. It was a thick, purple smoothie that smelled like blueberries. "Honestly, everything has been weird today. Sorry, I don't have time for this, though. I have to call to get Hailey Haddie a hotel in Fransmere for tomorrow. I love it there; I know she will too."

Ellie was so distracted by the smoothie that she hardly heard what Misha was saying. The smoothie was purple and gooey—just like the mystery goo. She spilled a cold glob on her hand and rubbed it between her fingers. Her heart sank. It wasn't sticky enough. Marilyn said the purple goop could have glued someone's lips together.

"But Hailey Haddie is supposed to be here tomorrow," Jessica said. "We know because we have a special invitation to be on set with her."

Misha shook her head. "Nope, unless the mystery of the purple goo is solved, the director is moving the movie at six tonight." She pulled out a paper with a bunch of numbers on it. "There it is!" She took the drink back from Ellie.

Ellie's shoulders slumped. "The play today and now this!? This isn't just the worst day ever; it is turning into the worst week ever. I won't get to meet Hailey Haddie now." She looked at a clock on the wall. It was almost four-thirty.

Jessica rubbed Ellie's back. "Maybe we can meet her in Fransmere. I'm going to go grab you a snack to cheer you up! Stay here."

Ellie dug her notebook out and updated it.

Clues

1. *Mysterious purple goop.*

Suspects

1. *Some sort of ghost – Wants people out of the house?*
2. *Marilyn Grin (makeup art) – Called director "crazy." Maybe wants some sort of revenge?*
3. *Misha May (assistant) – Seems happy to go to Fransmere.*

"Where is Fransmere anyway?" Ellie asked.

The assistant rezipped her backpack. "About six hours from here." Ellie's lip quivered. If the set moved, there was no way she would get to see Hailey Haddie tomorrow. Misha squinted at the set pass hanging around Ellie's neck.

"Wait, that set pass is for tomorrow. You're not supposed to be here," she said.

“NO! NO! NO!” shrieked a woman from across the house.

POOF!

The loud sound scared Ellie. And she wasn’t the only one startled—Misha jumped, making her smoothie go flying. Ellie transformed into a bat just in time to get a face-full of purple smoothie.

POOF!

Ellie shook the drink off her wings and transformed back into a vampire. Her hair was streaked with dripping, purple smoothie.

“Worst. Day. Ever,” she groaned.

Chapter Four

Déjà Vu

Ellie followed the crowd to a small room off the side of the living area. Tink and Fez were already there balancing plates piled with food. And Jessica was standing on the other side of the crowd. Inside the room were racks stuffed with costumes, towers of boxes overflowing with scarves, and shelves full of hats. A woman with short pink hair and red glasses knelt on the floor beside a pile of dresses dripping with purple goo.

"What happened?" Ellie whispered to Tink and Fez.

"The spooky house seems to have struck again," Fez said, his cheeks stuffed with food. He looked like the chipmunk statue in the yard. But far less creepy.

A man with a thick mustache, a ball cap, and a blue jumpsuit pushed a mop around to clean the goo off the floor. Ellie recognized him as the man who had signed in after her. It wasn't long before the goo glued the mop to the floor. He tugged the mop so hard that it ripped the head right off.

"Going to need more soap," the man grunted before pushing his way through the crowd. A sweet, flowery scent filled Ellie's nose as he walked past her—it reminded her of Ava's perfume project. She watched as he pushed a rolling cart into a door with a sign that said *Kitchen*. Coffee cups with lipstick on the rims clattered as the cart rolled through the door.

"All of these are ruined," cried the woman on the floor, looking at the gooey pile of clothes. Ellie couldn't see the woman's badge, but she had a feeling she worked for the costume department. "I left for just a few minutes and came back to all of these ruined dresses. So much work gone to waste."

"Including mine," came Ava's voice behind Ellie.

"Woah, déjà vu," Tink said.

"Huh. What does that mean?" Fez asked.

Ava's lip trembled. "It means that you feel like you've been in this same situation before. And that's exactly how I feel. I not only had to walk in to see my perfume smashed on the floor but now this! That dress with the flowers took me almost a week to hand-paint! I guess I don't get to be a finalist for anything. . . ." She glared at Ellie. "And why is it you and your friends are always around when it happens!? I know my brother Jack is mean to you, but I've been nothing but nice." Ava broke into tears and ran away.

Ellie was speechless. And the whole crowd was now looking at her, including the costume lady with the pink hair.

"So you are behind this!" the costume lady yelled.

"No, I didn't do anything," Ellie said.

"Then why are you covered in purple goo?" The woman turned to a man with a shirt that said SECURITY. "Escort her out!"

"But she didn't do it!" Fez said.

"Yeah, she was one of the last people to get here," Tink added.

"We're just here to see the set," Jessica said.

"Your badges aren't even for today!" Misha tattled.

The costume woman pinched the bridge of her nose. "Fine," she said in a calmer voice. "Then kick all four of them out."

"But we have a meet-and-greet with Hailey Haddie tomorrow," Ellie explained.

The woman snorted. "Not anymore. Take their badges! The last thing Hailey wants is vandals on set." The group was stripped of their badges and escorted out the back door. It slammed behind them with a *BANG* and locked with a *CLICK*.

"I didn't do it! I promise," Ellie said as they followed the path back down toward the guest house. "This is just smoothie on me. It isn't even sticky enough to be the goo."

"Of course it wasn't you," Jessica said. "You wouldn't have had enough time from where you were."

Ellie turned to Jessica. "But you had enough time."

Jessica's mouth fell open. "What? Ellie, you can't really think that."

"But Ellie, Jessica was with you," Fez said.

"No, she left to get me a snack right before it happened. And it's kind of convenient that Ava's dress was the one that got ruined. Jess, you even said you were mad that Ava's dress was picked and yours wasn't. You were jealous."

Jessica stomped her foot. "I did not ruin her dress! I'm not that mean. I still think mine was better, but hers had some nice material. Don't you believe me?"

Tink pushed his glasses higher on his nose. "Yes… but we were at the snack table the whole time and didn't see you."

Jessica's eyes widened. "So you don't believe me? We have a much bigger mystery to solve. A mystery that, if we don't solve it, we don't get to meet Hailey Haddie. But sure, let's focus on this."

Ellie gasped. Everything had happened so fast, she'd hardly had time to realize she wouldn't get to meet her hero tomorrow. Without her set pass, she wouldn't be allowed back in the mansion.

Jessica looked at all three of them with a trembling lip. "I went to the bathroom down the hall, so I never made it to the snack table before the costume fiasco. Some friends you are."

"We never said we didn't believe you," Ellie said. "You just definitely had access and motive—two things a suspect needs. Even Hailey's new book says that."

"I'm pretty sure that book didn't say to not trust your best friend!" Jessica huffed before storming off toward the mansion.

"Wait, Jess," Ellie said, running after her. Suddenly, the nearby guest house's window flashed white and blue. Ellie stopped but couldn't see anything through the dirty window.

Could a ghost be behind this? she thought to herself. By the time she looked back up, Jessica was gone.

Chapter Five

The Z Sisters

Ellie, Tink, and Fez peeked through the guest house window. There were holes where the oven and fridge used to be, and some of the cupboards were painted with graffiti. A wooden chest was pushed against one of the walls. Above it hung a painting of a cowboy rat.

"Are you sure you saw a ghost in here?" Tink whispered.

"I think so," Ellie said. "There was a flash of white like when ghosts appear and disappear." She pointed to muddy footprints leading to the front door. "Look."

"But why would a ghost leave footprints?" Fez asked. "Can't they just float?"

"And those look more like a cat or something," Tink said.

"Ooo, there's a cat?" Fez exclaimed. He rushed to the footprints.

"Sometimes ghosts leave glowing footprints," Ellie said. "But these don't look very glowy."

Fez sighed. "Tink, these are definitely not a cat.... The toes are too pointy. And cats only have four toe pads—this little guy or girl has five."

Tink shrugged. "I'm not always right." They followed the footprints to a crack beside the old house's entrance. They pushed the door open, but the footprints got lost on the dark brown floor. They stepped into a small room with only a desk and a sofa with a blanket and pillow. Ellie pulled out her magnifying glass as she sifted through some newspapers on the desk. One had a photo of the clown parade that had come through town last week.

"Looks like someone has been here recently," she said. "This newspaper is from a few days ago." She recognized it as the same

one the guard had been reading earlier. Suddenly, the floor creaked behind them. They swiveled around, but no one was there. Ellie gulped and turned back to the table.

"And look what's under it," Fez said. He grabbed the leather journal with the name *Zora* carved into the front. A silky orange ribbon was tied around the book. Ellie put her magnifying glass down and untied the bow before taking the journal from Fez. As she thumbed through the pages, the blueberry smoothie that had dried on her hand stuck to the paper.

"Do you think this belongs to *the* Zora?" Tink asked. "Like one of the famous Z sisters?"

"Who are the Z sisters?" Fez asked.

"They're pretty famous around here," Tink explained. "Remember how the town celebrated Witch's Week last month? It's a celebration of the Z sisters, AKA Zora, Zena, and Zee—the first three witches to come to Brookside. At first, the farmers were against them moving here and had a big plan to chase them out of town. But then they noticed that since the witches had moved to town that the big drought ended and their food was growing again. So instead of chasing them away, they invited them to a big supper in their honor. That supper became tradition and has been held every year since in the town square. The Z sisters are now ghost-witches, but they still attend every year."

"What's a ghost-witch?" Fez asked.

"Just a witch that died and became a ghost," Tink said.

"Actually, they have a special combo of

powers," Ellie said. "They can't do magic with wands anymore but can still make magic objects using potions. They can also go invisible and teleport through puffs of smoke, like a ghost. Oh, and some are psychic. Then again, that might just be the Z Sisters."

"That's so cool!" Fez exclaimed. Ellie flipped to the last entry in the journal. It had the same date as the newspaper.

"Look at this," she said. "Dear Claustra—" Right as she read the first words out loud, the orange ribbon from the diary wrapped around her wrists like handcuffs and the book fell to the floor with a *SLAP*. The ribbon's ends magically grew longer and wrapped around Ellie's body next.

"Help!" Ellie shrieked. The ribbon wound tighter.

"What is that!?" Tink asked as he tried to tug her free. No matter how much he and Fez pulled, the ribbon continued to tighten.

POOF! Ellie transformed into a bat. She tried to flutter away from the ribbon, but it followed her like a flying snake. It wasn't long before it was wound around her once again, pressing her wings to her sides. She tried to break through it, but it was stronger than her bat wings. She fell to the floor with a small thump.

Chapter Six
Enchanted Diary

Ellie tried to cry for help, but the ribbon was now wrapped around her mouth. She rolled on the guest house's floor like a bat burrito. Fez scooped her up in his hands.

"We need scissors or something!" Tink cried. He dug at the pile of stuff on the table like a dog digging a hole. There were no scissors in sight.

"Wait! There are scissors back in the theatre," Fez said.

"That's too far," Tink said. "We need to find something here."

Ellie's heart thumped in her ears, and her breath came in raspy. She knew this ribbon had to have been enchanted to trap anyone who read the diary, but she didn't know how to get out of it. She tried to turn back into a vampire, but she was panicking too hard. She took a few deep breaths to calm herself down and concentrated. *One, two, three*, she counted in her head. She tried to transform again, but she was still a bat burrito. *One, two, three,* she tried again, this time slowing her breathing. Finally, it happened.

POOF!

Growing sixty times her size in a second busted the ribbon into bits of orange confetti.

She transformed back into a vampire—just in time to see Jessica come running through the door.

"There was another mystery accident on set!" Jessica explained. "I was sitting on the other side of the house, and I kept hearing a strange beeping inside. Then, there was this big crash."

"Okay, but Jess—" Fez said.

"I looked in the window, and the entire food table was on the ground," Jessica continued. "The maintenance guy was cleaning the mess. He was also already there when I got on the scene with the ruined dresses."

"We have another problem right now!" Ellie exclaimed. She pointed to the orange bits of ribbon dancing in the air. One by one, they began piecing themselves back together. The ribbon was quickly whole again and snaking toward Ellie once more. Jessica snatched it out of the air, and it turned on her, binding her wrists together.

"Where did you find this?" Jessica asked. "What word did you say to make it come to life? You need to say the same word to make it stop." The ribbon flew over her mouth so she could no longer talk. She tried to shake the relentless ribbon off, but it was coiling farther down her body. Tink and Fez tried to pull it off of her, but it started to wrap around them too.

"It was in a diary. I was reading an entry," Ellie explained. She scrambled to her hands and knees to find the diary on the floor. The ribbon caught her ankle and tried to pull her toward her tied-up friends. She kicked it away and grabbed the diary. Her hands shook as she flipped through the pages. "All I read was 'Dear Claustra.'" The ribbon became limp and slunk to the floor.

"It was enchanted," Jessica said, kicking the ribbon into the corner. "That C-word probably activated it. Whatever is in the diary, someone doesn't want you to read."

They all gathered around the diary and silently read the entry.

Dear Claustra,

I saw him again today, lurking around the house. I hate how he keeps interrupting my vacation! I come here to relax, not to get my photo taken! I know, I know, he was probably just a reporter wanting photos of the movie set. He was carrying around some weird camera.

Sometimes I wish the mayor never agreed to let them film a movie here. Ugh, I can't wait until this is done. The sooner, the better.

Hmm, I wonder where Wally went...

Zora Zimmer xo

There was a drawing of the strange camera underneath the entry. It was a small box with a long antenna.

Ellie read over the name again. "Zora Zimmer. Definitely a Z sister!" She grabbed her notepad and updated her suspect list. She also copied the drawing of the camera.

Clues

1. *Mysterious purple goop.*
2. *Zora's diary and a newspaper. She was here not long ago. Where is she now?*

Suspects

1. ~~*Some sort of ghost – Wants people out of the house?*~~
2. *Marilyn Grin (makeup art) – Called director "crazy". Maybe wants some sort of revenge?*
3. *Misha May (assistant) – Seems happy to go to Fransmere.*
4. *Zora Zimmer – Wants her vacation spot quiet*

As Ellie finished in her notebook, a loud creak came from behind a wooden door. It had a soccer-ball-sized hole in the bottom corner. Ellie, Tink, and Fez all froze.

"Do you think it is Zora?" Fez asked.

Ellie looked at Tink. "You should go find out."

"Why me!?" Tink said, a little too loud. Crashing and clattering came from inside the closet. Through the hole popped two glowing eyes the size of peaches.

"Guys, I don't think that's Zora," Fez said.

"We should get out of here," Tink suggested. Everyone agreed. But before they could make it out the door, an explosion of white-and-blue smoke blocked the way.

Ellie shrieked. *POOF!* She transformed back into a bat.

In front of them stood a woman with wavy blue hair, a long flowy dress, and black gloves.

"What are you kids doing here?"

Chapter Seven

Woman in Blue

The three friends stood in silence as the woman with blue hair stared at them. Ellie flapped her wings above them.

"I said, 'What are you doing here?'" she asked a little louder.

POOF! Ellie rejoined her friends as a vampire.

The woman's face was turning red until her gaze fell on Ellie. Suddenly, a smile appeared. "Oh, hi, Ellie!" she said.

Ellie gave a small, shaky wave. "Hi, Zora."

"Wait, you two know each other?" Fez asked.

"Sure do," Zora said. "I met her during Witch's Week. Now, for the last time, what are you doing here?"

Ellie pointed to the closet and gulped. "Right now, running from whatever is growling in there."

Zora looked at the closet, listened for the growling, and laughed. "Wally, that is quite enough!" she said. She clapped her hands loudly, and the growling stopped.

"Who is Wally?" Jessica asked. Zora opened the closet door, and an avalanche of stuff slid out. There was everything from cupcakes to tin cans. A movie script poked out the top, along with some camera equipment from the movie set and green sunglasses. Zora reached into the pile and pulled out a fat raccoon. He had a round belly, a striped tail, and tiny hands with five fingers that clutched a magnifying glass. His eyes looked huge through it.

"Hey, that's mine!" Ellie said. She looked at the table where she left her magnifying glass last, and it was gone. Zora plucked the magnifying glass out of the raccoon's hands and gave it to Ellie.

"Sorry," Zora said. "Wally is a bit of a

thief. We're working on it." She plunked the raccoon down on the floor and took off her black gloves. "So much fur," she complained. She wiped the gloves off before stuffing them in her pocket. Wally scurried over to Fez and began sniffing his pockets.

"Aw, I think he likes me!" Fez said.

"All animals seem to like you," Jessica said. Fez pulled some fruit out of his pocket and gave it to Wally. "And that could be why," Jessica added with a giggle.

"Now, what are you doing here?" Zora said.

"The movie set is in the house, not out here. This is the only quiet place I have right now. Especially with the other half of the guest house being used for your school presentations."

"Is that why you're trying to scare everyone away?" Ellie asked. "To get the house to yourself again?"

Zora's eyebrows slammed together. "What? No. Of course not. I am really sorry about Wally's growling. He just gets protective of his treasures." She glanced at Fez, who was playing with the tubby pet raccoon. It waddled away into the kitchen.

"Wait, I just want to pet you," Fez said, chasing after Wally with outstretched arms.

"I think Ellie is talking about the mysterious things that have been happening on set," Jessica said.

"I have nothing to do with that," Zora said.

"We know you want your vacation place to be quiet again," Tink said. "We read your diary."

Ellie's face turned red with embarrassment. "Just the last entry!" she added.

Zora groaned. "Did the silly enchanted ribbon not work? Look, I don't love that this place is busy. But the movie set actually saved this old house from being demolished." She went to grab the newspaper off the table, but her hand went right through. "Whoops, forgot my gloves," she said. She pulled a pair of plain black gloves out of her pocket and slipped them on.

"Why do you need winter gloves to read the paper?" Tink asked.

"They're GGGs—ghost grab gloves," Zora explained. "They let me grab objects. As you saw, without them my hands just float right through stuff." She grabbed the newspaper off the table and flipped it open to an article with a picture of the house. The headline read: *Old House Saved by New Movie in Town*. The article explained that if the house wasn't used for something by the end of the year, they would tear it down.

"So the movie needs to happen here, or you'll lose this spot?" Ellie asked.

"Exactly. I don't want things to go wrong,"

Zora explained. "I've been inside trying to figure out what's happening, but no luck. I kept hearing a weird beeping. I think it might have been coming from the loft, but I'm not sure."

"I heard it too!" Jessica said.

Ellie crossed Zora off her suspect list. "Then I think we need to get inside and try to find that beeping," Ellie said.

"How?" Jessica asked. "They kicked us out after those dresses got ruined." She lowered her voice to a mumble. "And you guys don't believe it wasn't me."

"Do you have proof you were in the bathroom when the dresses got ruined?" Ellie asked.

Jessica exhaled sharply. "Are you kidding me? You've known me forever. I shouldn't need to give you proof."

"Good detectives always need proof," Ellie said.

"I didn't realize good detectives equaled bad friends," Jessica grumbled. "Fine, how's this for proof? In that bathroom, there was a weird painting of a pirate chipmunk. How would I know that if I wasn't in there?"

"That doesn't really prove anything, because I haven't been in that bathroom. I don't know if there is a painting or not," Ellie said. "You might just be saying that because there is a pirate chipmunk statue outside."

Jessica crossed her arms. "Then it looks like we have two reasons to get back into that house."

"But how are we going to get back in there? We can't just go invisible like Zora," Tink said.

Fez came back into the room, holding Wally like a baby in his arms. "I have an idea."

Chapter Eight

Master of Disguise

Fez led Ellie, Tink, Jessica, and Zora to a wooden trunk in the kitchen. The beady eyes of the cowboy rat in the painting above it gave Ellie the chills.

"I found this while chasing Wally," Fez said. He popped open the chest to reveal a pile of old clothes and costumes. "We can disguise ourselves."

"This is great… but they won't let us in the door without set passes," Tink said.

"That's okay. I have another idea of how to get in," Fez said. "Trust me."

Ellie started digging in the trunk.

"Oh sure, trust him," Jessica mumbled. All four of them pulled on bits and pieces from the trunk. Ellie wore overalls and a ball cap, making her look like a mini maintenance man. Jessica found a leather jacket and sunglasses. And Fez found a long coat with a hood. He tied a rope around his waist as a belt.

Ellie updated her notebook and briefed everyone on what she had written so far.

Clues

1. *Mysterious purple goop.*
2. ~~*Zora's diary and a newspaper. She was here not long ago. Where is she now?*~~
3. *Mysterious beeping – What is it?*

Suspects

1. ~~*Some sort of ghost – Wants people out of the house?*~~
2. *Marilyn Grin (makeup art) – Called director "crazy". Maybe wants some sort of revenge?*
3. *Misha May (assistant) – Seems happy to go to Fransmere.*

4. ~~Zora Zimmer – Wants her vacation spot quiet~~
5. *Maintenance Man – Always first on the scene?*

"It's suspicious that the maintenance guy was one of the first on the scene for the broken food table and ruined dresses," Ellie said as they waited for Tink to change.

"Agreed, but it is his job to clean up," Jessica pointed out.

"I think I've made a mistake," Tink said. He wore an orange bodysuit with a furry hood that had two googly eyes. "I thought it was just long sleeve overalls! But it's a lion costume."

Zora smirked. "I think you look like the *cat's meow*. And I'm not *lion*." Everyone laughed.

"You guys are enjoying this way too much," Tink groaned.

"At least no one will recognize you," Ellie said.

"Can't I change into something else?" Tink asked. Ellie looked at the watch on his wrist that read 5:00.

"No, we only have an hour to figure this out," Ellie said. "Let's go!"

"Good luck," Zora said with a wave.

"Aren't you coming?" Ellie asked.

Zora shook her head. "I wish I could. But I have a meeting with the mayor in a few minutes." She scooped up the tubby raccoon. "But you've got this! I had a vision of Ellie acting on that movie set tonight, so I know you can do this. I'm counting on you all. Good luck." Wally gave a small wave as both he and Zora disappeared in a puff of smoke.

Ellie snorted. "Yeah, right. I'm never acting or getting on stage again."

Jessica mumbled something under her breath.

"Maybe she got you confused for Hailey Haddie," Fez said. "You two do have the same hair."

Ellie blushed. "Thanks, Fez! That's the best compliment ever."

Tink sighed as he swished his tail. "Now what?" he asked.

"What do chipmunks, foxes, rats, and groundhogs all have in common?" Fez asked. "Besides that they're super cute!"

"They're... brown," Jessica guessed.

"They were all made into creepy lawn statues," Ellie said.

"Close!" Fez said.

"They all have tails?" Tink guessed.

"Yes, but all those animals also make tunnels underground. And Ellie taught me to look for hinges on the side of paintings and stuff. You know, for secret doorways. Well..." He pulled on the painting of the rat, and it swung open like a door. "Tada!"

The three friends gasped.

"Wait. So you figured this all out because they're burrowing animals?" Tink said. "You might be the genius in this group."

"Sometimes it pays to know about cute animals!" Fez said. Tink grabbed his flashlight out of his backpack and popped it on. They crouched into the portrait hole and walked down a set of steps. The sound of dripping water echoed through the rocky tunnel. The

air was moist and heavy.

"ACHOO!" Jessica let out a loud sneeze and turned into a rat. The tunnel crumbled slightly. Ellie couldn't help but smile. She was happy she wasn't the only one with transformational powers she couldn't control. She was also thankful she didn't transform every time she sneezed. She scooped up furry Jessica and plopped her in her overall pocket. To her dismay, Jessica bit her finger.

"Ow!" Ellie cried. A large rock fell from the tunnel's ceiling right behind them. Jessica scurried into Fez's coat pocket.

"Shh!" Fez said. "The tunnel did not like that."

"Jessica shouldn't have bit me," Ellie complained. Tink shone the flashlight at a hatch in the ceiling.

"Now, I bet you we will pop out right at the rat statue," Fez said. Cool fresh air flooded their noses. Fez was right. "Now let's go find the chipmunk's entrance and get back into that house!"

Chapter Nine

Ohio Girl

Ellie stood inside the mansion's bathroom. She stared at the painting of the pirate chipmunk. Jessica was right. And she felt awful for ever doubting her.

"Jess, I'm sorry," she said to the sweater-wearing rat sitting in Fez's pocket. "I should have believed you. I'm just trying to be a good detective… but that should never mean being a bad friend."

Jessica let out a small squeak and hopped into Ellie's overall pocket. Ellie took that as Jessica accepting her apology.

"The coast is clear!" Tink said, peeking out the bathroom door. The four friends slunk against the wall to the loft ladder. Then, when no one was looking, they climbed up one by one. The loft's walls were lined with dusty books and records. And in the corner was a mattress on the floor.

"What's beside that record player?" Ellie asked, creeping toward the silver music box in the corner. Fez bent down and picked up an apple. It had one single bite taken out of it.

"Looks like this apple was recently eaten," Fez said. "I know because the white part inside is only a little bit brown. The longer an open apple sits, the browner the inside gets."

"That's because of oxidation," Tink explained. "If you want to stop it from oxidizing, you need to add something with vitamin C, like lemon juice."

"That makes sense!" Fez said. "I forgot to add lemon juice to a fruit salad once. All the cut apples ended up looking like they got a suntan."

Ellie giggled. The apple really did look like it had a suntan where the bite mark was. She turned her head as she analyzed the spot. "Does anyone remember a person missing a fang today?" she asked. Everyone shook their heads. "This bite mark only has one fang indent. Whoever was up here is missing a fang."

"Ooo, that's a good find!" Fez said.

Fez shoved the apple toward Tink. "Put it in your backpack."

Tink wrinkled his nose. "Ew. No. I am not putting someone's half-eaten apple in my backpack. Isn't it enough that I'm dressed like a lion?"

"It's evidence," Ellie said. "We need to keep it."

Tink grumbled as he zipped open his backpack and popped in the apple. Next, they scanned the rest of the loft for clues on who it might belong to. There were lots of old books on jewelry making and cooking. But the one that caught Tink's eye was a book of old maps.

"Woah, can you believe Brookside used to only be half as big? It is so small on this map." Ellie touched the book, and the page stuck to her hand.

"Don't dirty the book," Tink said, wiping off the smudge she'd left behind. If there was one way to offend Tink, it was by harming a book.

"Sorry, my hands are still all gunky from that blueberry smoothie," Ellie explained. She held out her sticky hands.

"Do you think maybe that sticky purple goo around the set is smoothie?" Fez said. "I know when I forget to clean the blender out after making a smoothie, it gets pretty sticky."

"No, I tested the smoothie earlier, and it wasn't sticky enough..." Ellie said, but then she paused for a few seconds. "But it was a fresh smoothie! You're right, Fez. Old smoothie is much stickier. Maybe that assistant, Misha May, is behind this, because she wants the movie set to relocate. She seemed excited about going to Fransmere."

Tink flipped to another page. "This place here," he said, pointing to a map of Ohio with a Fransmere label in the corner.

Ellie gasped. "I think Misha is from there! She had a sticker on her backpack that said Ohio Girl. No wonder she wants to move the filming location there. We need to go question her. Now."

The four friends only moved a couple steps before the floor fell out from under them. Their screams echoed as gravity yanked them down a long and twisty slide that funneled them into darkness. They landed in a heap at the bottom with a *THUMP* and *CRUNCH*.

Chapter Ten
Secret Passage

Ellie, Tink, and Fez lay in a clump at the bottom of the mysterious slide. Ellie felt her pocket for Jessica, but she was gone.

"I heard a crunch. Is Jessica okay? Is everyone okay!?" Ellie shouted. Her voice echoed through the blackness.

"Yes, but I can't see a thing," Tink answered.

"The crunch might have been me crushing a book," Fez said. "Sorry, Tink." The sound of a zipper opening vibrated through the thick air. Tink shone the flashlight at Fez and grabbed the book. It had a string hanging out the side.

"I think we found another secret passage," Tink said. "And Fez opened it by pulling out this book." He moved the flashlight across the small room with no windows and cobwebs blanketing almost every surface. A workbench stretched across the back wall opposite a tall, narrow mirror.

"Jessica? Where are you?" Fez called. A small squeak came from the workbench. Jessica sat beside a small bowl of metal nails, rusty pliers and hammers, spools of wire, and bits of metal.

"Oh, thank goodness!" Ellie said. They continued to look around the room, but there was no exit anywhere.

Ellie groaned. "How are we going to get out of here? We need to go see Misha, that assistant. We have less than an hour before they move the set. Or we lose our chance to spend time with Hailey Haddie."

Jessica squeaked. Tink followed her with the flashlight to a small hole in the wall. She squeezed in with a butt wiggle and disappeared.

Fez gave a little squeal. "She is just so cute as a rat!"

Ellie and Tink laughed. A few seconds later,

Jessica scurried out of the hole.

"A-a-achoo!"

POOF! She transformed back.

"Sanalamia," Ellie said. "And welcome back."

"I tried to go through the wall to find a way out, but all the dust made me want to sneeze. And what if I transform back in a small space like that?" Jessica said. No one knew exactly what would happen, but they knew it couldn't be good. A metal star dangled from Jessica's hand.

"What is that?" Ellie asked. Tink shone the

flashlight at it.

"Looks like an earring," Jessica said. "I found it in the wall." She held it up to Ellie's ear before plopping it into Ellie's overall pocket. "It's pretty cute. Too bad I only found one. Maybe the other is around here somewhere."

"I found a vent!" Fez said, pointing to the ceiling. "Ellie, you can fit if you transform into a bat."

Ellie examined the small opening with a dusty grate. "But how are the rest of you supposed to get out of here?" she asked.

"Maybe you can find a way to get us out after you save the movie. I don't want you to miss Hailey Haddie," Jessica said. The boys both agreed.

"No way! I would never leave you guys. We're a team," Ellie said.

Fez's mouth fell open. "Wow, did you just say you pick us over your all-time hero?"

Ellie gave a big, fangy smile. "Yup. Hailey Haddie's amazing, but solving mysteries with you guys is my favorite."

Tink grinned. "Rat Jessica is pretty great."

"Ooo, I agree!" Fez exclaimed.

"Hey! What about normal me?" Jessica huffed.

"Good, but it's hard to beat a rat," Tink teased.

Jessica exhaled sharply. "You can be a lot sometimes."

"Plus, rat Jessica isn't all sassy. She just gives cute little squeaks," Ellie joked.

"Exactly!" Tink said.

Jessica rolled her eyes and laughed. Tink's flashlight flickered. He dug in his backpack and yanked out the bitten apple, books, wire, and goggles.

"Is there anything you don't have in there?" Jessica asked.

"Yes," Tink said as he pulled out a notebook and potatoes. "Extra batteries. If the flashlight dies, we will be stuck in the dark."

"Let's just find a way out before it dies," Fez said.

The flashlight flickered off, blanketing the basement in darkness.

Ellie gulped. "Too late."

Chapter Eleven

Reflection

The four friends stood frozen in the middle of the pitch-black basement. The air felt extra damp and heavy in the dark.

"How are we going to find a way out with no flashlight?" Ellie asked. "We need light."

"Did anyone see any candles?" Fez asked.

"No, but I'm surprised Tink didn't have any in his backpack," Jessica said. "He even has potatoes! Raw potatoes."

"Those aren't even mine!" Tink said. "Fez must have put them in there."

"Hey, it wasn't me!" Fez said.

"Actually, that was me..." Ellie said. "I needed some potatoes to make stamps for our Jellyfish Lake play props. But I asked if I could put them in there, and you said yes! Although, you were busy doing a science project at the time."

Tink gasped. "That's it!"

Jessica smacked her lips. "Tink, I know you can't see my face right now, but it isn't impressed. I don't think potato stamps are getting us out of here."

"No, not that," Tink said. "I know a science experiment that can help us. I just need two pennies and two nails. I already have the wire, potatoes, and the lightbulb."

"I have two pennies!" Fez said. Change jangled in his coat pocket.

"And I saw nails on the bench," Jessica said. She felt her way to the workbench and grabbed the bowl full of nails.

"Great! Ellie, I need you to unscrew the flashlight and take out the lightbulb," Tink said.

"On it!" Ellie said. She took the flashlight from Tink and did as she was told. With some clinking and clattering, soon the basement flooded once more with light.

"You did it!" Jessica cheered. "I don't understand how this works, but it works!" On the ground were two potatoes, each with a penny and nail sticking out of them. Wires ran from the nails and pennies to around the lightbulb's base.

"It's a light that runs off the energy from the potato. I did it as a science project before. The acid in the potatoes reacts with the metal to allow electrons—"

"Tink, we need to find a way out of here," Ellie said. "Can you explain all this later?"

Tink grinned. "Sure can! You can read my report on it. It's only eighty-one pages."

They circled the room a few times. Eventually, they were all drawn to the mirror. Tink moved his hips side to side, making the tail in the back of his costume wag in the mirror.

"I don't love this disguise, but this tail is kind of fun," he said.

"Lucky," Fez said. "Next time, I want to be the cat." He wiggled his butt, but his coat just swayed slightly. Next, he twisted his hands into the shape of a bunny and created a shadow

puppet on the wall. "I may not have a cool cat costume, but I can make cute bunnies," he said. As Fez made his bunny hop around, he bumped a wire out of place on the potato light. The room went dark again. "Whoops," he said. Tink fixed the wire, and the light started back up.

"Hey, cat and bunny, shine the light up here," Ellie said. The light swept to the top of the mirror with carved words. She wiped the cobwebs off. "Exit. Get out of your way to get out."

"What does that even mean?" Jessica asked. No one knew. They tried to push aside the mirror. Then they tried to push on the glass, but nothing happened. Next, Ellie checked for hinges around the side to see if it swung open, but there were none.

"It just looks like a plain mirror," Fez said.

"How do you get out of your own way to get out?" Ellie said.

Tink scratched his chin. "Hmm, maybe your reflection blocks the way. Like some sort of magic mirror." The potato light flickered.

"I've heard of that before!" Jessica said. "If that's true, this is a super rare mirror. A witch used to make them, hoping to help vampires escape from humans hunting them. The idea was that vampires have no reflections, so they could step through, but humans can't."

"But you guys do have reflections," Tink said. "I saw Ellie's today."

"Exactly," Jessica said. "It wasn't very

useful, so only a handful were made."

"If everyone has a reflection, does that mean there is no way out of here?" Fez asked.

"I'm not sure," Jessica said. "The only reason I know that story is because it's an old vampire legend."

Fez put his hand on the mirror. The potato light flickered and then went out completely.

"Woah!" yelled Fez. After Tink fiddled with the wires, the potato light came back on. And Fez was gone.

Chapter Twelve

Wanted

Tink shone the potato light around the dark basement, but Fez was nowhere to be seen.

"Fez? Where did you go?" Jessica asked. Ellie paced back and forth in front of the mirror and pushed her hand against the cold glass. It was solid.

"Fez. Fez!" she called in a shaky voice.

"I'm here," said a muffled voice from the mirror. Ellie jumped back.

"You got through?!" asked Tink. He ran up to the mirror and touched the glass. "How?"

"I don't know," Fez said. "But wherever I am, it's very dark, so please hurry with the potatoes."

"That's it!" Ellie said. "He got through in the dark. If it's dark, you don't have a reflection. Turn off the potato light." With one pulled wire, the light turned off, and Ellie stepped through the mirror. Jessica and Tink followed.

"It worked! Good solve!" said Jessica. The potato light flickered back on. A narrow brick hallway stretched in front of them. At the end was a staircase that led to a hatch with light creeping through the cracks. Ellie gently pushed it up and climbed through. Then, one by one, they emerged in a small closet.

"I hear something," Ellie whispered. Swishing water was only a few feet away from them.

"On the count of three, we get out and face whatever it is," Jessica said. "One, two, three." The four friends burst out of the closet into a bathroom.

Misha screamed at the surprise, dropping the pile of clothes she was holding into the pink tub. They were caked with purple smoothie.

"Aha! We caught you red-handed," Ellie said.

"Or should we say, purple-handed," Tink corrected.

"Don't tell the costume department about this!" Misha begged. "I was in charge of cleaning the costumes, but I slipped and spilled some smoothie. Now they're even more stained. I can't afford to get fired." The lines in Misha's face softened. "Wait a second, didn't you all get kicked off the set earlier? I'm calling security!"

"Go ahead," Jessica said. "We will just show them proof that you have been sabotaging the set all day. We know you want the film set to move to Ohio."

Misha frowned. "What? I just spilled some smoothie. I have nothing to do with the other incidents." She turned to Ellie. "I was with you when those dresses got ruined, so how could I be the one who ruined them? I wouldn't risk my job just to go to Ohio. I've been trying to save money to go back and visit my family for a long time. And I will never have enough if I get fired...."

"But you won't need money if the filming is

in Ohio," Ellie said.

Misha snorted. "Not true. They live on the other side of Ohio. There is no way I would have time to go see them with how busy it is on set. The only time I ever get off is Christmas, so I am trying to save enough money to fly there before then."

Fez approached the purple-stained clothes in the tub. He scooped some smoothie with his finger and licked it. Then he did the same with the purple goo.

"These are two different things," he said.

"The purple goo tastes more like honey."

Ellie crossed Misha off her suspect list with a sigh. Jessica looked at the purple-stained clothes floating in the tub.

"How about we make a deal? If I help you clean these clothes, you pretend you didn't see us," Jessica said.

"I don't think there is anything that can get these stains out," Misha said.

"Yes, there is," said Fez. "Jessica knows this super-secret stain formula that works like magic! She gave me some, and it gets everything out! Paint, juice, spaghetti, you name it."

"Okay. It's worth a shot," Misha agreed. Ellie looked around the small bathroom. She took in the cracked tiles and the pink bathtub, but it was a discolored piece of paper by the door that caught her eye. It had yellow tattered edges and handwriting in black ink. It looked very old. Ellie caught a whiff of perfume and coffee as she picked it up.

WANTED: MOTHMAN

7-foot-tall monster with milky skin and bulging

red eyes. May have wings spread out but can also hide them. Leaves behind a trail of purple slime. Lets out a squeaky screech when it hunts.

Last seen in Brookside mountains.

Ellie's hands shook as she finished reading the paper. She updated her notes.

Clues

1. *Mysterious purple goop.*
2. ~~*Zora's diary and a newspaper. She was here not long ago. Where is she now?*~~
3. *Mysterious beeping – What is it?*
4. *Wanted Poster for Mothman*

Suspects

1. ~~*Some sort of ghost – Wants people out of the house?*~~
2. *Marilyn Grin (makeup art) – Called director "crazy". Maybe wants some sort of revenge?*
3. ~~*Misha May (assistant) – Seems happy to go to Fransmere.*~~

4. ~~*Zora Zimmer – Wants her vacation spot quiet*~~
5. *Maintenance Man – Always first on scene?*
6. *Mothman – Lives here and doesn't want people around?*

She showed everyone the flyer. "Anyone see a giant moth man or hear a squeaky hunting cry?"

"I heard a squeaky screech come from the entryway when we got here!" Fez remembered. "But you would have seen him; you were still signing in."

Ellie thought back. "You probably just heard me step on the maintenance man's toes." She read her suspect list over once again. "Which means he can't be behind this, because purple goo incidents were happening before he got here." She crossed his name off the list.

"That means that Mothman is our new lead," Jessica said.

Tink threw his backpack over his shoulder. "Then let's go find him."

Chapter Thirteen

Lights, Camera, Action

Ellie, Tink, and Fez snuck around the house as Jessica helped Misha. It was already five-thirty. They only had thirty more minutes to solve this case, or they wouldn't get to see Hailey Haddie tomorrow. And from the old wanted poster Ellie had found, they were now on the hunt for a monster called Mothman. If the Mothman had settled in this house while on the run, it would make sense that he was trying to get people out.

"We should go ask Zora if she has seen any winged monsters around," Tink suggested. "She's spent enough time here." They went to check the guest house, but Zora wasn't there.

Back in the main house, they tiptoed from

room to room. There was no purple goo or sign of a giant winged monster. They peeked around a corner into the living room, where a movie scene was being shot.

"Let's get this one over with so we can get out of here!" said a man sitting in a director's chair with a megaphone. He ran a hand through his black, slicked-back hair before clutching a bulb of garlic hanging on a necklace.

"Guess he doesn't know that garlic is to get rid of vampires and not ghosts," Tink mumbled.

Ellie rolled her eyes. "It doesn't even get rid of us. It's just gross, so we prefer to avoid it."

"I don't think it gets rid of Mothman either," Fez gasped. "Look!" He pointed to a winged shadow on the wall. It stood towering behind the two actors on set, and no one seemed to notice.

"We have to save them!" Ellie yelled. She pulled her monster spray out of her pocket and ran onto the set.

"Wait," Tink cried, but it was too late. Ellie ran around set in her overalls, spraying the

lavender monster spray. She looked around for who was casting the giant shadow but couldn't spot them.

"Cut! CUT!" the director yelled. "What on earth are you doing?" The shadow disappeared.

"The Mothman," Ellie said. "He was right here. I saw his shadow. He's the one who has been sabotaging the set all day!" The shadow flickered back on the wall. "Look!" she cried. She turned, and there was still no Mothman. But there was a woman holding a bat doll in front of a light to create a wall shadow.

"Oh," she mumbled. All of the actors, camera people, sound crew, costume department, and a ton of other people were staring at Ellie. Her heart started beating harder, but she had to save the movie. She took a deep breath and hopped up on the sofa. She waved her flyer in the air as she stood on the cushions like a brown, flowery stage.

"Okay, so that wasn't Mothman. But we're on the hunt for him," she explained. "He's seven feet tall, with milky skin and bulging eyes." She flapped her arms by her side. "He may have wings spread out, leaves behind slime, and lets out a squeaky screech." She tried to make a screechy sound, but it came out more like a bird squawk. "Okay, I don't know how the monster sounds, but it might be something like that."

The director walked up to Ellie and snatched the flyer out of her hand. "Let me see that!" he sneered. All the color drained from his face as he read the flyer. "We're done!" he shouted. "Wrap it up now. I don't want anything else to do with this haunted house."

"If we catch him, it will be fine," Ellie explained. "And I think I hear him. Listen!" A low growling came from nearby. "Do you hear that?" Ellie whispered. Everyone froze. She followed the sound right to Fez.

"Unless the Mothman is in Fez's stomach, that isn't a monster sound," Tink whispered.

"Never mind," Ellie said. "But he must be here somewhere!" The movie crew scattered and wasn't paying attention anymore.

"Sorry, but something smells like coffee cake," Fez said. "And I am getting hungry."

Ellie turned back to the director, but he was already running out the door. The flyer fluttered to her feet.

"Wait!" she yelled, but the director was gone. She picked up the poster. "You're probably smelling the wanted poster," she said to Fez. "I noticed earlier it kind of smells like coffee." She turned the poster over, and her heart sank. "And now I think I know why." On the back was a flyer for the Witch's Week festival—the one that had happened only a couple weeks ago. There was no way it was a real old wanted poster if that was printed on the back.

Her voice caught in her throat. "This isn't some old wanted poster. I bet someone planted this to throw us off the trail. They stained it with coffee to make it look old… And I fell for it! We just wasted almost all of the time we had left because of me. I'm so sorry."

Fez patted Ellie's back. "We didn't notice either." He sniffed the paper again. "The paper also smells like perfume, sort of like Ava's. Do you think maybe she is behind it?"

"No," Ellie said. "Why would she want to ruin her own dress? She seemed pretty upset. And that purple goo makeup incident happened before we got here. We saw Ava just before we left the guesthouse, so how would she have had time to do that?"

Misha popped her head into the room. "The director just demanded the rest of the set get packed up. Any luck?" Ellie shook her head, and Misha offered a small smile. "You gave it your best shot."

Ellie slumped her shoulders. Now she wouldn't get to spend time with Hailey

Haddie, and Zora's vacation spot would probably be torn down. She knew even great detectives didn't solve all their cases. But she still felt like she had failed.

Chapter Fourteen

Behind the Curtain

The four friends stood in the living room that now just had a few lights and some furniture left.

"The take-down crew sure does move fast," Tink said. Ellie looked at the empty set. It was just the four friends and the maintenance man taking down the lights. Everyone else was packing up the trucks outside.

"This has still been a fun day," Jessica said. But Ellie wasn't paying attention; she was too busy analyzing her detective notepad. She scratched out Mothman and sighed. She couldn't believe she had fallen for a fake clue. She'd thought she was getting to be a better detective, but now she wasn't so sure.

Clues

1. *Mysterious purple goop.*
2. ~~*Zora's diary and a newspaper. She was here not long ago. Where is she now?*~~
3. *Mysterious beeping – What is it?*
4. ~~*Wanted Poster for Mothman*~~

Suspects

1. ~~*Some sort of ghost – Wants people out of the house?*~~
2. *Marilyn Grin (makeup art) – Called director "crazy". Maybe wants some sort of revenge?*
3. ~~*Misha May (assistant) – Seems happy to go to Fransmere.*~~
4. ~~*Zora Zimmer – Wants her vacation spot quiet*~~
5. ~~*Maintenance Man – Always first on scene?*~~
6. ~~*Mothman – Lives here and doesn't want people around?*~~

"The only person left on the suspect list is Marilyn Grin, that makeup art lady," Ellie said. "But there was no evidence pointing to her doing it. And she left before two of the purple goo incidents."

"You mean, makeup artist. Not makeup art," Jessica corrected.

"No, her set badge said 'makeup art,'" Ellie said.

"Hmm, that's weird," Jessica said. "You sure?"

Ellie thought back to the woman in the car. "Maybe not…her long hair was on top of part of her badge." She went to the sign-in sheet and scanned it for Marilyn's name. There it was, right on top. "Marilyn Grinko! Do you think she is related to Jack and Ava?"

"If she is, then why would she ruin Ava's dress?" Jessica said. "And like you said, she was gone before that happened anyway."

Ellie looked down at her overalls, Fez's coat, Jessica's leather jacket, and Tink's lion costume. "Unless she came back in disguise!" Ellie said. She ran back to the living room and pointed to the cart. "And those cups with old coffee could have been used to stain the wanted poster," she whispered.

Fez smiled. "I think we just blew this case wide open." The mystery team walked over to the disguised Marilyn Grinko. Her face was makeup-free, but up close, Ellie noticed a few sparkles were still stuck to her eyelids from her earlier eyeshadow.

"Excuse me, Marilyn," Ellie said. Marilyn looked up at the sound of her name and then immediately back down.

"No. No Marilyn here," she said in a deep voice. Jessica pulled back the curtain that skirted the bottom of the cart. Underneath was a huge container of purple goo and the camera that Zora had drawn a sketch of.

"We know you're behind the set sabotage," Ellie said. "And now we have proof. But why?"

Marilyn ripped off her fake mustache. "Fine, you caught me. I wanted everyone out because I'm looking for a very valuable piece of jewelry here. This whole movie was in the way."

Fez pulled out the camera from the bottom shelf. "Then what do you need this for?" he asked.

"Don't touch that!" Marilyn said in an icy voice. "That's a custom detector used to find magical objects." A red light flashed on, and it started beeping.

"Oops," Fez said.

"That's the beeping sound I heard!" Jessica said. Marilyn snatched the machine away and turned it off.

"Now leave," she said.

"No way!" Jessica shouted. "Once we tell on you, the movie will stay here."

Marilyn cackled. "And who will believe you? You're just a bunch of troublesome kids who snuck on set."

"I will!" said a voice from the loft. Hailey Haddie was standing at the top of the ladder. She took a few steps down the rungs before they broke. She crashed to the ground with a small scream, and Marilyn took off running.

Chapter Fifteen
Confession

Ellie and her friends rushed to Hailey Haddie's side. She was standing now, rubbing her butt. One of her fangs sat on the floor beside her.

"Are you okay?" they asked.

"Yes, but she's getting away!" Hailey pointed to Marilyn, who was running out the front door.

"Get back here!" Ellie yelled. She chased the woman out to the front of the house. Marilyn ran down the winding steps of the mansion. Ellie couldn't believe how fast the older woman was. The gap between them was growing bigger and bigger each second.

"Marilyn, get back here!" Ellie yelled. Just

as Marilyn zipped past the fox statue, a lasso rope snagged her. She jerked to a stop.

"Ah, get this off me!" she yelled. Fez was holding the other end of the rope.

"No way!" he said.

Ellie gasped for breath. "Fez, how did you beat me here?" she asked.

"The last tunnel!" Fez said. "The fox painting was sitting right above the snack table."

"And the lasso?" Ellie asked.

"Something I learned on the farm as a kid."

"Let me go!" Marilyn screamed.

"Grandma?" said a boy's voice. Jack and Ava came running to Marilyn's side. Ellie gulped. The last thing she needed was to deal with Jack right now.

"Are you okay?" Ava asked as she loosened the lasso.

"No, this pesky vampire and her friends tied me up," sneered Marilyn.

Jack's face turned red. "They did what?"

"No, Marilyn. Er—your grandma? She has been sabotaging the movie set all day. She even ruined your sister's dress!" explained

Ellie.

"Ava came home crying today, and she told me that YOU ruined her dress," Jack growled.

"That's because it *was* her!" Ava said.

"No, it was your grandmother. Honest!" Ellie said.

Ava looked down at Marilyn. "She's lying. Right?"

Marilyn's gaze trailed to the ground. "No… but it was an accident! I didn't know that your dress was in that bunch. I feel so, so awful. I would never do that to you on purpose, Ava."

A tear rolled down Ava's cheek. "I want the perfume I made back!"

Ellie realized that the flowery perfume she had been smelling all day was Ava's creation after all. Ava walked past her grandma and over to Ellie.

"I'm sorry I accused you." Ava glared back at her grandma. Then, she pulled a purple necklace out of her pocket. "I found this today beside your jellyfish costume backstage." Ellie patted her neck frantically. She hadn't even noticed her favorite dragon necklace was missing.

"Oh my goodness, thank you!" Ellie said as she put her necklace back on. "I was so panicky, I didn't notice it fell off." She gave Ava a monster hug. "I'm so sorry about the perfume and your dress."

Ava gave a small smile. "It's okay. Mr. Bramble said I don't need the perfume to do my presentation. As for the dress, that wasn't your fault. My family can be… a little crazy sometimes."

Tink came running outside. "Hailey Haddie

just called the director and explained everything. Filming here is back on!"

Ellie gave a squeal of excitement before she noticed Jack and Marilyn were walking away. It didn't matter, though. They'd solved the mystery and saved the movie.

Once back inside, Ava and Ellie were promptly greeted by Jessica holding Ava's purple-stained dress.

"My dress is the only one from the competition that didn't get ruined," Jessica said.

Ava sighed. "I suppose I should say congratulations then. Your dress *is* nice."

"Wait, I'm not done," Jessica said. "I want to cut up your dress."

Ava frowned. "Was getting stained purple not enough!? Now you want to completely destroy it?"

"No, I want to help you rebuild your dress using mine. Your fabric is beautiful, and it deserves to be seen. But we only have a couple hours before the scene, so we have to hurry!"

Tears filled Ava's eyes. "Wow, you guys are so nice. I'm glad I gave that necklace back."

Ellie wasn't sure what Ava meant about the necklace. But before she could ask, Jessica whisked Ava away toward the costume room. Hailey Haddie waved at Ellie from the sofa.

"Come have a seat," she said. Ellie happily went to sit beside her hero. It felt like a dream. Hailey smiled—she now had both fangs.

"How did you get your fang back in?" Ellie asked. "It was on the floor when you fell." Hailey grabbed the fang with her fingers and popped it out.

"It isn't real. I lost my real fang falling off a

teeter-totter as a kid."

"You were the one who ate the apple in the loft!" Ellie realized. "Why were you here so early?"

"Nice detective work," Hailey said with a wink. "Yes, that was me. I take my fang out when eating apples, so it doesn't get pulled," Hailey said. She lowered her voice. "Between you and me, I get really nervous starting new projects. I like to get on set early and find a quiet place to rest before. I do deep breathing and picture myself being successful on the project. It helps to calm my nerves."

Ellie smoothed out her overalls. "I get really nervous in front of large crowds of people. Today I tripped during a play. Everyone laughed."

"Oh my, that's rough," said Hailey Haddie. "But you also stood up in front of a huge group of people and told them all about the Mothman. I was watching from the loft, and it was a wonderful performance."

"I never thought of it that way," Ellie said with a small smirk. "I guess it *was* like a performance."

"Sure was," said Hailey. "Plus, you saved the movie and solved a mystery. You have to focus on the positives of the day."

"And I got to spend time with you!" Ellie added. "You know, somehow this turned from one of the worst days to the best."

Hailey smiled. "I'm glad to hear. Is there anything I can do to repay you for saving the movie?"

Ellie looked over at Misha, who was hauling camera equipment back inside.

"Can you get Misha May home to see her family?"

"I can absolutely do that! And can I maybe ask one thing of you?"

Chapter Sixteen

The Show Must Go On

Ellie jiggled her jellyfish tentacles behind the heavy red curtain. She counted to four as she inhaled, then did the same as she exhaled. She thought about how the night before she had been an actress on a real movie set. After the fall, Hailey didn't feel well enough for her night scene. But it needed to be shot that night at the eclipse. Ellie stood in, since she had the same brown hair and the scene was shot from behind. She had to stand on a box to be the right height, but she did it. And with everyone watching! She still couldn't believe it. She even got to keep the dress that Ava and Jessica had made for the scene.

Ellie took another deep breath. Ava and

Lily had already presented their perfume made with flowers from the lake. Then, Luke and Gopher talked about how jellyfish were important to the lake's food chain. Now, the sound of Tink and Fez finishing up their presentation carried backstage. That meant she and Jessica were next.

"And that is how jellyfish mucus might be able to fight pollution in our water," Tink said.

"Fish snot to the rescue!" Fez exclaimed with a huge grin. The audience broke out into applause. Ellie closed her eyes and pictured the audience doing the same for her and Jessica.

Jessica stood beside Ellie. "You okay?"

Ellie nodded. "I think so." Her heart was pounding, and her palms were soaked with sweat. But she didn't want to quit. They had come too far.

Jessica smiled. "You can do it, Ellie. I believe in you!"

"Next up, we have Jessica Perry and Ellie Spark," boomed Mr. Bramble's voice over the microphone. "This is their original short play,

The Mystery of the Missing Jellyfish."

The curtain lifted, and the spotlight once again found Jessica. The room was even more packed than the day before, with more chairs added to the rows. There were even parents standing along the walls. Ellie's heart skipped a beat as she scanned the crowd—Hailey Haddie was standing among them.

"I am so excited to visit Jellyfish Lake," Jessica said. She pretended to walk by the lake. "I can't wait to see all the jellyfish. Oh, there is one! But where are all of its friends?"

The spotlight swooped over to Ellie. She took a step forward—but not before looking down to make sure there were no tentacles in the way.

"Hello, jellyfish, where are all your friends?" Jessica asked.

Ellie took a deep breath and stood tall. "My friends went missing yesterday," she said. "Will you help me find them?"

"Of course," Jessica agreed. They went on to save the jellyfish, and their play was almost done. Then, suddenly, Ellie's foot hit something slippery. She slid on a puddle of Fez and Tink's jellyfish mucus and fell.

"Ellie fell! Scaredy bat fell!" laughed Penny, Ellie's little sister. Mrs. Spark hushed her. To Ellie's surprise, no one else was laughing.

Ellie got to her feet. "Wow, who knew jellyfish mucus was so slippery?" she said. She looked down at her costume. "Oh, I guess I should have known. After all, I am a jellyfish!" The room exploded with laughter. This time, Ellie laughed too.

The play resumed and soon came to an end.

Ellie let out a sigh of relief and took a bow as the audience gave them thunderous applause. After the room quieted, Mr. Bramble stepped onto the stage with the six other finalists.

"Well, that was quite the show!" he said. "Where you found such an imaginative idea, I will never know."

Ellie, Jessica, Tink, and Fez all looked at each other and giggled. The play was loosely based on what had really happened to them at the lake last month. But no one else knew that.

"However, only one team will win these two tickets to Mega Adventure Land," Mr. Bramble said. He waved two white paper envelopes in the air. "So, without further adieu, the winner is..." He ripped open one envelope. "Tink and Fez, with their presentation on jellyfish mucus! Congratulations." The two boys jumped for joy as they grabbed the ticket envelope.

"I can't believe we won!" Fez said once they were backstage.

Jessica laughed. "Well, your team is made up of a genius and a great presenter."

"Aw, you think I'm a genius?" Fez joked, batting his eyelashes. Jessica laughed again and rolled her eyes. Ellie slunk down a wall onto the wood floor. She wasn't laughing or smiling like everyone else.

"Are you mad you didn't win?" Tink asked. "Because I thought you were going to! Your presentation was so good."

"Super-duper good!" said Fez.

"Yeah, Ellie, we did really well. Don't be mad," Jessica said.

Ellie shook her head. "I know, I'm not mad we lost. You two deserved to win!" She twirled her glowing dragon pendant around her finger. "I just wish there were enough tickets for all of us to go. Also, this costume is a million degrees. I really need to change."

"Sorry," said Jessica. She held out her hand to help Ellie up. "Next time, I won't use so much rubber."

Ellie let out a loud sigh. "You know, I feel bad for rubber ducks. They must be super hot all the time." Everyone laughed.

Ellie went into the bathroom and changed.

Once she had a breezy dress on, she splashed her face with cold water. She looked in the mirror and smiled. She couldn't believe it. She had faced her fear of being onstage. A loud cheer from the hall tore her away from her thoughts.

Ellie ran out to see Jessica, Fez, and Tink jumping around.

"There are four tickets!" Fez said. "You and Jessica can come with us!"

Ellie squealed. "No way!"

Tink showed her the four amusement park tickets. "I don't know how it happened," he said. "I could have sworn Mr. Bramble said there were only two."

Jessica bounced up and down. "Best. Week. Ever!"

"Wow, wish come true!" Ellie agreed. She'd faced her stage fright, saved the Hailey Haddie movie, and now she got to go to the opening of the new amusement park. It turned out being a Scaredy Bat was pretty amazing with the right friends by your side.

Ellie punched the air in excitement. "Mega Adventure Land, here we come!"

Are You Afraid of Public Speaking?

Glossophobia [glaa-suh-fow-bee-uh] or stage fright is the intense and persistent fear of public speaking. It comes from "glossa," the Greek word for tongue and "phobos," the Greek word for fear.

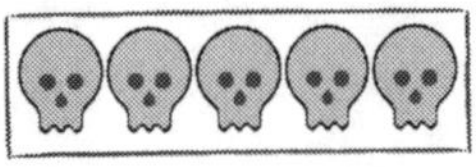

Fear Rating: Glossophobia is one of the most common phobias. People with this phobia can experience shaking, sweating, dry mouth, stiff back, and rapid heartbeats.

Origin: Fear of public speaking is a social phobia that may be caused by genetics, a negative past experience, and fear of being judged, embarrassed, or rejected.

Fear Facts:

- Formal public speaking originated in Ancient Greece as part of democracy.
- People are more afraid of public speaking than death, spiders, and heights.
- The Guinness World Record for Longest Speech was awarded to Ajay Shesh in 2015, who spoke for over 60 hours on how to become a better person.
- U.S. President Franklin D. Roosevelt said: "Be sincere; be brief; be seated."
- Tips: Know your topic, practice, visualize, embrace pauses, and breathe.

Jokes: Did you know there are public speaking potatoes? *Nothing special really, they're just commen**taters**.*

Fear No More! With preparation and practice, most can conquer public speaking fears. But if you believe you suffer from glossophobia and want help, talk to your parents or doctor about treatments. For more fear facts, visit: scaredybat.com/bundle2.

Suspect List

Fill in the suspects as you read, and don't worry if they're different from Ellie's suspects. When you think you've solved the mystery, fill out the "who did it" section on the next page!

Name: Write the name of your suspect

Motive: Write the reason why your suspect might have committed the crime

Access: Write the time and place you think it could have happened

How: Write the way they could have done it

Clues: Write any observations that may support the motive, access, or how

Suspect 1

Draw below

Name:	
Motive:	
Access:	
How:	
Clues:	

Suspect 2

Draw below

Name:
Motive:
Access:
How:
Clues:

Suspect 3

Draw below

Name:
Motive:
Access:
How:
Clues:

Suspect 4

Draw below

Name:
Motive:
Access:
How:
Clues:

Who Did It?

Now that you've identified all of your suspects, it's time to use deductive reasoning to figure out who actually committed the crime! Remember, the suspect must have a strong desire to commit the crime (or cause the accident) and the ability to do so.

For more detective fun, visit:
scaredybat.com/bundle2

Name:
Motive:
Access:
How:
Clues:

Hidden Details Observation Sheet

-- Level One --

1. What does Ellie dress up as for her school play?
2. Who do Ellie and her friends hope to see at the movie set?
3. What was Misha the assistant drinking when Ellie first met her?
4. Which of the kids wears a lion costume as their disguise?
5. What vegetable does Tink use to create a light?
6. Who is hiding beneath the maintenance man disguise?
7. What does Ava give back to Ellie that she had lost?
8. How does Fez stop Marilyn Grinko from getting away?
9. What fear does Ellie overcome in this book?
10. What tickets do Tink and Fez get for having the winning presentation?

Hidden Details Observation Sheet
-- Level Two --

1. Why does Ellie's class perform at the mansion theater instead of at school?
2. What is in the bottle that Ellie accidentally smashes behind stage?
3. Where would the filming move to if they couldn't solve the mystery?
4. What gets spilled on the clothes in the costume room?
5. What does the maintenance man smell like?
6. What creature left the footprints leading to the front door of the guest house?
7. Who was eating the apple in the mansion loft and left a single fang mark?
8. How do Ellie and friends get out of the basement?
9. Who is featured on the wanted poster Ellie found in the bathroom?
10. What does Ellie slip on during the Parents' Night presentation of her play?

Hidden Details Observation Sheet
-- Level Three --

1. What kinds of animals are the statues in front of the mansion?
2. Who do the kids find staying in the guest house of the mansion?
3. What phrase activates the enchanted ribbon on the diary?
4. What does Zora the ghost-witch use to grab objects?
5. What does Jessica hear coming from the loft?
6. Behind which painting do the kids find the first secret passage?
7. What object do the kids accidentally pull that opens the passage into the basement?
8. What is the movie director wearing around his neck to protect himself?
9. What is on the back of the fake wanted poster?
10. What is Marilyn Grinko looking for in the mansion?

Answer Key

Level One Answers

1. A jellyfish
2. Potato
3. Hailey Haddie
4. Purple (blueberry) smoothie
5. Tink
6. Marilyn Grinko, Jack and Ava's grandma
7. Her purple dragon necklace
8. Public speaking / Stage fright
9. Mega Adventure Land tickets
10. With a lasso

Level Two Answers

1. Fake jellyfish mucus
2. Perfume made from Jellyfish Lake flowers
3. Fez and Tink accidentally flooded the school gym
4. Fransmere, Ohio
5. Purple goo
6. Flowery sweet perfume
7. Wally the raccoon
8. Hailey Haddie
9. Through the magic mirror
10. Mothman

Level Three Answers

1. Chipmunk, fox, rat, and groundhog
2. Zora; one of the Z Sisters witches
3. Dear Claustra
4. Ghost Grab Gloves
5. A mysterious beeping
6. The Cowboy Rat
7. A book
8. Garlic
9. The witch's week festival flyer
10. A valuable magical piece of jewelry

Discussion Questions

1. What did you enjoy about this book?
2. What are some of the themes of this story?
3. How did the characters use their strengths to solve the mystery together?
4. If you could go behind the scenes of a movie set, which one would you choose?
5. How did Ellie overcome her stage fright?
6. Tell me about a time you presented in front of a group that you're proud of.
7. If there were a secret passage in your home, where would it be?
8. What other books, shows, or movies does this story remind you of?
9. What do you think will happen in the next book in the series?
10. If you could talk to the author, what is one question you would ask her?

For more discussion questions, visit:

scaredybat.com/bundle2

Scaredy Bat

and the Mega Park Mystery

By Marina J. Bowman

Illustrated by Paula Vrinceanu

CODE PINEAPPLE

Contents

Batty Bonuses

Can you solve the mystery?

All you need is an eye for detail, a sharp memory, and good logical skills. Join Ellie on her mystery-solving adventure by making a suspect list and figuring out who committed the crime! To help with your sleuthing, you'll find a suspect list template and hidden details observation sheets at the back of the book.

SMOOTHIE
SHACK
ADVENTURE EATS
MEGA ADVENTURELAND

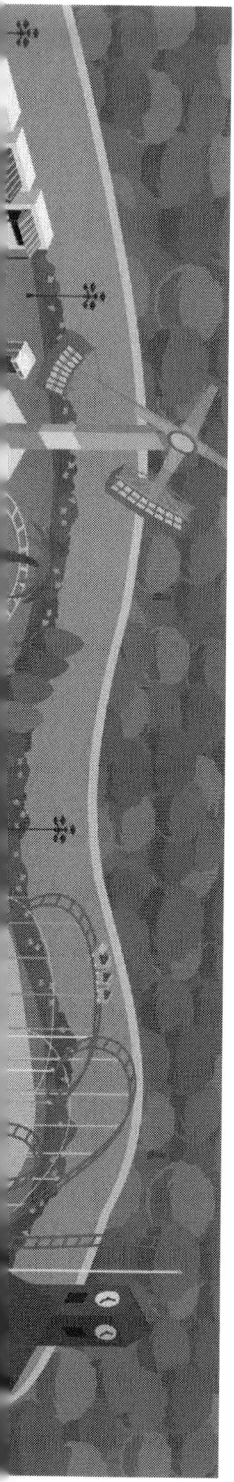

There's a place not far from here
With strange things 'round each corner
It's a town where vampires walk the streets
And unlikely friendships bloom

When there's a mystery to solve
Ellie Spark is the vampire to call
Unless she's scared away like a cat
Poof! There goes that Scaredy Bat

Villains and pesky sisters beware
No spider, clown, or loud noise
Will stop Ellie and her team
From solving crime, one fear at a time

Chapter One

Lost and Found

Ellie was trapped in the dark, humid cocoon. The harder the twelve-year-old vampire twisted and turned, the more stuck she got. She took a deep breath of the stuffy air and groaned. "Where is it?"

"Woah, did you know that Mega Adventureland has the world's tallest roller coaster?" asked a muffled voice beside her. "And did you know they grow special flowers that taste like candy and fresh-baked dessert?"

Ellie wiggled, feeling like a giant worm. "Did you know you aren't being very helpful?"

"Whoops," Tink said. He tugged the blanket cocoon and it rolled off the velvet sofa with a soft thump. Ellie's mess of long, tangled hair spilled on the yellow rug as she inhaled the fresh air.

"Now, keep looking," she instructed as she straightened her glasses.

Tink sighed as he put the pamphlet down on the stained-glass end table. He ran his hand through his short, curly hair as he glanced around the earthy-colored living room. "Can't we do this later?" he asked. "Jessica and Fez will be here any minute."

"No way!" Ellie said. A half-empty bag of beet chips from her sleepover with her sister the night before crumpled under her knee. She groaned as small red shards spilled onto the floor. She wasn't looking for a snack. Although, a mysterious, fruity smell was making her tummy rumble. Tink popped open the old wooden trunk that doubled as a coffee table.

"I'm sure you have other jackets and necklaces," he said. "We're going to an amusement park, not a fashion show."

"That's not the point!" Ellie said as she peered behind the caramel-colored TV stand. "I need that necklace. I've worn my purple dragon pendant every day since my grandma gave it to me for my tenth birthday. I'm telling you, it's lucky! And we need all the luck we can get today." Her stomach bubbled with excitement thinking about the grand opening of the Mega Adventureland amusement park. She was excited for the rides and food, but most of all, she couldn't wait for the Mega Mystery Mansion.

"True, we could use some luck today," Tink agreed. "I can't wait to see Jack's face when we solve the Mega Mystery Mansion before him and win the bet." Ellie smiled at the thought of beating the mean boy in her class. Not only would she be ten dollars richer, but maybe then Jack would finally see what a great detective she was.

"We better win," Ellie added. "I bet my allowance. To earn it, I had to clean the attic to help my mom make room for her art studio. There's no way I inhaled a hundred pounds of dust and, like, ten spiders just to give that money to Jack!"

"Um, you eat spiders all the time," Tink reminded Ellie. "On purpose!"

Ellie slid her tongue over her pointy fangs. "Okay, but they aren't the same when they're dusty! It dries out their juiciness. Now keep looking so we can win that bet!"

Tink exhaled dramatically as he crawled behind the sofa. "What does the jacket look like again?"

"It's a turquoise trench coat with a plaid band," Ellie said crawling behind the sofa from the other side. "I know I put my necklace in the pocket yesterday before raking leaves." She found Penny's blue knit sweater, a rubber duck, and a jellyfish stuffed animal behind the sofa, but no jacket.

Tink turned his nose up in the air and sniffed like a dog. "Mmm, it kind of smells fruity back here. Like oranges," he said.

"I know!" Ellie said, inhaling deeply. "I smelled that earlier too. I can't figure out what it is though. It reminds me of Stinky Lou's invisibility formula. I remember the smell from when I had to figure out who was sending me that mystery invitation."

Tink giggled as he backed out from behind

the couch. "Oh, yeah! That was a lot of fun. But are you ever going to stop accidentally calling him Stinky Lou? We fixed his sunscreen so it doesn't smell anymore."

Ellie chewed her cheek as she stood. "I know. I'm trying," she said. And she meant it. She knew that Tink idolized Lou. The local scientist had become his friend and mentor after they'd met a couple months ago. They were always working on science experiments together, picking each other's brains on new theories, and often indulging in ice cream.

"Did you guys ever figure out how to make that invisibility formula stop smelling like oranges? I mean, it kind of defeats the purpose if people can smell you."

Tink shook his head and sighed. "I haven't seen Lou in awhile. We were working on how to get his formula to stop smelling, but that was weeks ago. It's like he doesn't have time for me lately..." Tink's shoulders slumped.

Ellie patted his back. "He's probably just got something going on right now. I'm sure you'll be back to working on your science-y stuff together soon."

"Hopefully," Tink said. He turned to his friend, and his mouth fell open. "Ellie, I think that smell is coming from your hair." Ellie's hand shot up to her head. A sticky lump the size of a cherry was nested in a clump of her brown strands.

"Oh my goodness, what is this!?" she exclaimed. She rushed toward the mirror in the hallway and shrieked at the sticky mess. "There's a lollipop stuck in my hair!" She gave it a quick tug, and a sharp pain shot through her scalp as a huge tuft of her locks tried to go with it.

"Don't pull!" Tink advised. "I have an idea." He grabbed his backpack and pulled out a jar of cinnamon and a book with orange four-leaf flowers on the cover. It was called *Gnome Sweet Gnome: Cooking with Magic Plants.* He dug out lots of science stuff, too, but he didn't stop until he found a bottle labelled '*Fitzgerald's Slick and Sweet Salad Dressing.*'

Ellie wrinkled her nose. "What are you going to do with that?"

"Put it in your hair," Tink answered.

"I was afraid you were going to say that." Ellie sighed and bent her head down to Tink. "Are you sure this will work?"

Tink drizzled the sticky nest of hair with the dressing. "It should. The oil in the dressing will counteract the stickiness and help the lollipop slide out. It's either this or cut the lollipop and a chunk of your hair." He tugged the oil-covered candy.

"Ouch!" Ellie cried.

"Sorry. This is one sticky lollipop," Tink said as he tried to give it another tug.

"That's because they're made with yummy, yummy Lillup sap," said a small, cheerful voice. Ellie's little sister Penny stood in the doorway. She had chocolate-brown hair just like Ellie's, a turquoise plaid cape, and a big, fangy grin pasted on her round face. A colorful dragon kite dragged behind her.

"Fez dropped off a bunch of Lillup Lollys yesterday," Ellie explained. "They're really good, but super sticky. He said only gnomes know how to grow the plant that makes the

sap, so they're special."

Penny ran around the room as she giggled and pinched her nose. "Scaredy Bat smells like a stinky salad."

Ellie's face grew hot and red. "Go away!" she yelled.

"No, this is my house too!" Penny shouted back.

"Got it!" Tink exclaimed, holding the hairy lollipop in the air like a trophy. Penny plucked the sticky treat from his hand. After picking off the hair and wiping it on her turquoise cape, she popped it in her mouth.

"My jacket!" Ellie cried, pointing to the cape. Penny's eyes grew wide, and she bolted out the front door.

A snap of cold wind sent a shiver down Ellie's body as she ran outside after Penny. Her sister raced around the crunchy, leaf-covered lawn, her dragon kite slowly rising into the air. Its shiny scales gleamed against the dark clouds as it snaked through the sky with its streamers fluttering in the wind. Ellie gasped as a purple sparkle in the middle caught her eye.

"Give me back my dragon necklace!" she shouted.

"You'll have to catch me!" Penny taunted. She disappeared around the side of the house with her plaid cape flapping in the wind. The dragon kite and the necklace floated behind her.

Chapter Two

New Heights

Penny laughed as she circled the rusty swing set a few times and headed toward the old apple tree. Then, just as she passed the tree, she was snapped backward like a rubber band. Ellie's little sister flew into a giant pile of crispy leaves. She popped out a second later with twigs woven into her hair and tears flooding her eyes.

"You pulled me into a pile of leaves!" Penny screeched. "I'm telling!"

"I did not!" Ellie said. She pointed to the kite string dangling from the tree. It was surrounded by fake hanging bats and pumpkin lights from Halloween last month. "You got your kite AND my necklace stuck. That's what pulled you back."

Penny gasped. She jerked her head toward the kite jammed high in the tree. "You got my new kite stuck! I'm telling Mom. Mom! MOM!"

"Shh. Keep your voice down," Ellie said. "We promised Mom we wouldn't fight today so she can get her painting done for the gallery opening. You're going to get us both grounded. Remember what Dad said this morning after the beef and liver oatmeal fight?"

Tink's face turned a sickly green. "Beef and liver oatmeal?"

"We were fighting over the last bowl when... well, things got a little messy," Ellie explained. "We were told if we argue again today, we're grounded for two weeks." Memories of a tug-of-war for the last bowl of oatmeal flashed through Ellie's mind. She could picture her dad's face turning red as a tomato when the beefy breakfast food splattered onto the ceiling—and his new suit.

Penny smirked. "Yeah, but if you get grounded, you can't go to the park today." Ellie ignored Penny and grabbed the kite string with one hand and tugged, but it wouldn't budge. She yanked harder. Nothing. She gripped the string with both hands and tugged one more time—a ripping sound echoed from the top of the tree. The string puddled to the ground, but no kite followed.

Ellie cringed. "Oh no."

"You broke it!" Penny cried. "You ripped my new kite. MOM!"

A woman with dark hair pulled into a bun and paint-splattered overalls poked her head out of the back door.

"What is going on out here?" Mrs. Spark asked. Ellie's heart sank into her stomach. Penny was going to get her grounded. Then, she realized something that could save her.

"If you tell, you'll be grounded too, and your birthday party will be canceled," she whispered. "That means no park for you either." Penny's mouth fell open and she stood there in silence. She had been begging to go to the amusement park opening all week. She'd even tried to convince Ellie to take her by doing her laundry, which accidentally turned all of Ellie's white clothes pink. The only thing that stopped the begging was when their mom told Penny she could have her birthday party there next week.

"Penny? What did you need?" Mrs. Spark asked.

"Oh, um... Can I have a snack?" Penny finally answered. Ellie let out a sigh of relief.

Mrs. Spark squinted at the two sisters. "I am almost certain you two were fighting again. But you know what? I have a painting to finish. So if you are both good now, let's pretend this didn't happen. Agreed?"

Both girls looked at each other and nodded.

"Come on, Penny. Your friend Libby called earlier and left a message. Leave Ellie and Tink alone."

Penny ran inside, but not before sticking out her tongue at Ellie. The door closed with a click.

Ellie looked at her necklace dangling from the kite high in the tree. Then, she grabbed the rough bark of the lowest branch.

"What are you doing?" Tink asked.

"Saving my necklace!" Ellie answered. She pulled herself higher just as a strong gust of wind rustled the leaves.

"This tree is really high. Maybe we should get a ladder or something?" Tink suggested. "Or when Jessica gets here, maybe she can just turn into a rat and climb it." The sky darkened and gave a low rumble.

"That will take too long. What if it rains and the necklace gets ruined? Or a bird grabs it?"

"Then why don't you turn into a bat and fly up?" Tink asked.

"It's really windy, so it will be harder to fly," Ellie explained. "Plus, I'm an expert climber! I used to go up this tree all the time." She craned her neck to look at the kite and gulped. "But it was a lot smaller then," she mumbled. She shimmied along the branch to grab the next one and pulled herself up once again. Her hands grabbed branch after branch until she clasped the dragon kite's body. After she untangled the dragon's tail, it was free and floated to the ground with the necklace like a giant leaf.

"See, that wasn't so bad," Ellie said, sitting on a branch near the top.

"Great! Now you just need to get down," Tink said.

Ellie tried to move her leg down to the next branch, but it felt like a giant, wobbly spaghetti noodle. She remembered that to get down from the tree, she always turned into a bat and flew to the ground. She closed her eyes, getting ready to transform.

WHOOSH! A gust of wind whirred through the tree, shaking Ellie off the branch.

"AHH!" Ellie yelled. Her fingers clasped around a branch halfway down the tree. She dangled from the limb, her sweaty fingers slowly slipping off. Her arms shook like electrified pool noodles as her fingers slipped further off the branch.

"Ellie!" Tink cried. But Ellie could barely hear him over her heavy breathing and hammering heart. It was a long fall to the ground.

SNAP! Suddenly, the tree limb broke.

"AHH!" Ellie shrieked as she rocketed downward. Everything became a blur as she tried to turn into a bat. With a crispy clunk, she plummeted into the giant pile of leaves below.

Chapter Three

My Detective Senses Are Tingling

"Ellie!" Tink dove toward the leaf pile that was taller than he was. He dug in the crunchy leaves like a dog making a hole. But no matter how many leaves he tunneled through, there was no Ellie. It was as if she'd disappeared.

"What are you looking for?" Fez asked as he skipped into the backyard with Jessica, a container under his arm. "Ooo, is it a squirrel!?" His rosy cheeks plumped as he squinted at the colorful leaf pile.

Jessica sighed. "Sorry we're late. *Someone* had to stop and watch every squirrel he saw on the way here. Where's Ellie? We have to get going."

"I don't know!" Tink said. "She fell from the tree and just disappeared."

"What do you mean she fell from the tree?" asked a wide-eyed Jessica. Both she and Fez bolted to the leaf pile to help with the search. A flurry of leaves whirled in the air as the trio dug.

"I got her!" Fez said. He pulled out a limp bat with a missing wing.

A shriek of horror came from Jessica. Followed by a groan. "Fez! That's just a Halloween decoration."

"I'm over here," said a muffled voice. A ghost-white Ellie crawled out of the other side of the pile. She slumped against the tree trunk and pulled her knees to her chest.

"Are you okay?" Tink asked. The three friends hugged the shaking little vampire.

Ellie nodded. "I think so. But I didn't turn into a bat. I always thought I would be able to turn into a bat on cue if I fell from somewhere high. What if there wasn't a big leaf pile to save me?" She groaned. "Guess I'll add heights to my never-ending list of fears. I don't want to fall from somewhere and break a million bones in my body."

"Technically you don't have a million bones in your body…" Tink started. Jessica glared at him. "But you could have gotten really hurt. I'm glad you're okay." They helped Ellie up. Her whole body was still shaking.

"I think I am going to skip the high rides today," Ellie said.

With a loud *THUNK!*, a tree branch crashed beside Ellie. *POOF!* She instantly turned into a bat and dove back into the leaf pile.

"Hey, at least you know your transformational powers still work," Jessica said.

POOF! Leaves exploded from the pile as Ellie transformed back into a vampire. She spat a twig from her mouth.

"Sure, now they work," Ellie groaned.

"Are you sure you still want to go to Mega Adventureland?" Fez asked.

"Yes," Ellie said. "And we should go before Penny changes her mind and tells on me for ripping her early birthday gift." She held up the tattered dragon kite.

"What happened?" Fez asked. "That poor dragon looks like it went through a shredder."

Ellie sighed. "It's a long story." She plucked her necklace from the kite and put it on.

Mrs. Spark popped her head out of the door again. "Ellie, before you go, can you come inside and talk to your sister? She won't stop crying and she won't tell me why." A tidal wave of guilt flooded Ellie's stomach. She hadn't realized that Penny loved her new kite that much.

Ellie found Penny sobbing behind the sofa in the living room. Eventually, Penny let out a squeaky sob that was broken up randomly with the words "Libby," "Park," and "Birthday." After she calmed down, they finally got the whole story. Penny's friend Libby had called with bad news about the amusement park.

"She said that her family only stayed for a half-hour because it was so boring. A lot of the rides and games are already broken! And more kept breaking, like, every few minutes." Her lip trembled. "Then she told me that I would have to cancel my birthday party because no one will want to go." Penny hugged her knees to her chest, and Ellie's stomach sank. Penny may be pesky ninety-nine percent of the time, but she was still her sister.

"What if I can go and fix it?" Ellie blurted before fully realizing what she was saying.

Penny's eyes grew wide. "You can do that!?" She crawled out and gave Ellie a huge hug. "That would make you the best big sister ever!"

Ellie ignored the confused looks from Jessica, Fez, and Tink.

"How are you going to fix broken rides?" Jessica asked as they got on their bikes in the driveway. "No offence, but you aren't very handy with tools."

Ellie shook her head. "No, but I can solve mysteries. And my detective senses are tingling."

Chapter Four

Mega Adventureland

The sound of screams from the roller coaster echoed blocks before the detective team got to the gate. And it wasn't long before the double loop and drop of the roller coaster came into view. A lump settled in Ellie's throat, making it hard to breathe. Her eyes trailed the twists and turns of the ride that wove through the right side of the park. She tilted her head back to take in the tallest peak that disappeared in the gray clouds. Her heart pitter-pattered faster at the thought of being up that high. There was no way she was getting on that ride. After falling out of the tree, she never wanted to be anywhere super high again.

Ellie brought her attention back to the bike

ride. The cold breeze carried the sweet smell of funnel cakes and donuts through the parking lot. She thought she heard the laugh of a clown in the distance, but it was hard to tell over her friends' panting. They locked their bikes to a stand and took their places in line in front of the rainbow gate.

Fez and Tink sat on the cold pavement, huffing and puffing loudly.

"It feels. Like my lungs. Are going to explode," Tink said between heavy breaths.

"I don't even think I have lungs anymore," Fez said with a cough.

"That's not possible," Tink panted.

Jessica laughed between heavy breaths. "Ellie sure does peddle fast when there's a mystery to be solved."

Tink pulled a metal bottle from his backpack. As he chugged the cool water, he pulled the gnome book and a sandwich from his bag.

His eyebrows slammed together as he held up the snack. "A sandwich? When did I pack a sandwich?"

Fez snatched the container. "You didn't. I

did!" He quickly ate half the strawberry jam sandwich, then offered the rest to the gang. Only Tink accepted.

"When did you even put this in my bag?" Tink asked as he took a big bite.

"When Ellie was talking to Penny in the house," Fez said. "I love your backpack!" He picked the gnome book off the pavement. "Hey, look!" He pointed to the orange four-leaf-clovers with spiky middles by the gate. "It's the same flowers as on the cover! Clover-tines! They must have hired a gnome gardener

for the park." Sure enough, a short gnome with bare feet, a star on his arm, and a red apron came out to water the flowers with a long hose.

"I wish this line would hurry up," Ellie groaned. She tapped her foot on the pavement as she counted how many people were in front of them. There were only five groups, but it felt like the line wasn't moving at all.

She peered through the rainbow arch entrance, the only opening in the tall metal fence surrounding the park. Through the colorful

archway was a concrete mermaid fountain filled with aqua water. Behind it, a colorful merry-go-round was spinning to a happy tune. Farther back sat a ride shaped like a giant spider with seats on its legs that scrambled around. No one seemed to be riding that one. The only person there was someone in a black sweater with their hood pulled up.

"Look," Ellie whispered. Everyone watched as the hooded figure climbed under the ride and then back out. The ride stopped, and the person disappeared behind a red building by the game booths to the right.

"Okay, I'll admit that was fishy," Tink said.

Ellie smirked. "Looks like we have our first suspect." She reached into her coat pocket and pulled out her detective notepad. A tiny drop of drool dribbled on the paper as she scribbled down suspects. It was hard to concentrate with the smell of fresh pretzels and tangy mustard wafting through the air.

Suspects

1. *~~Mustard~~ Mystery person in hoodie.*

"Look who is here," Jessica whispered. At the back of the line were Jack and Ava Grinko. Jack was Ellie's enemy, but his sister was one of her friends. "Once we solve this case, I can't wait to solve that big-house-mystery-thing to beat Jack," Jessica added.

Ellie giggled. "You mean, the Mega Mystery Mansion."

Jessica waved her hand dismissively. "That's what I said."

Ava gave an enthusiastic wave with the arm that wasn't cradled in a pink, sparkly sling. Ellie cringed thinking about when Ava fell in gym class and sprained her wrist. Before she could wave back, a giraffe-like woman stepped in front of Ava. The tall woman looked overdressed to be at an amusement park, with a long flowy dress, a leather jacket, and high-heeled boots. Her eyes were bright blue like Jack and Ava's, but her hair wasn't dark like the siblings; it was a frosty blond. Although, from the dark roots, Ellie suspected it was hair dye.

"Ugh, this place should be called Super

Loud Land," the woman complained. "If I can hear this ruckus from our house, I will have this place shut down in an instant!" The whole line turned to see who made the overly loud comment.

Jack's face flushed red. "Mom, keep your voice down. You're embarrassing me."

Mrs. Grinko rolled her eyes. "This is taking too long!" She strutted past the mystery team to the front of the line. Everyone caught a nose-full of the woman's strong peppery perfume.

Jessica pinched her nose. "Oh, sweet pudding. That is wayyy too much perfume."

The sound of Mrs. Grinko yelling at the ticket person echoed down the line. Both Ava and Jack pulled up their jacket hoods to try to hide their faces.

"I feel bad for them," Fez whispered. "Even for Jack."

The gnome gardener twisted his red moustache as he now stared at Ellie. His eyes were glued to her dragon necklace.

Ellie clutched the pendant, remembering

how gnomes loved to collect things that were their favorite color. She felt her stomach churn as he turned off the hose and approached her.

"Oh, that's a very special necklace," he said in a soft voice. "So rare. I've never seen one in real life. Be sure to take good care of it." Before Ellie could ask what he meant, her attention was snatched away.

BANG! A loud sound echoed from the gate. Ellie wondered for a second if Mrs. Grinko had literally exploded with anger. But the sound seemed to be from farther away.

"The sky is falling! The sky is falling!" screamed a woman from inside the park.

Chapter Five

Cotton Candy Disaster

The whole line shoved through the park gate to see what was happening inside Mega Adventureland. There were hundreds of golf-ball-sized pink and blue clouds floating from the sky. The ones that landed in the mermaid fountain instantly melted in the water.

"It's raining cotton candy!" Fez exclaimed.

Ellie, Jessica, Tink, and Fez stuck out their tongues, trying to catch the cotton candy snowflakes. One of the fluffy mounds floated into Ellie's mouth, and a burst of sweetness hit her tongue. She ran over to catch a blue one, which tasted surprisingly sour. Its tart fruitiness reminded her of the raspberry flavor of Jelly Belly Jam Jerky, a jam-filled meat snack.

She peered at the source of the sugary rain

shower—a cotton candy machine with a long wall the size of a car collapsed on half of it. With a good chunk of the machine crushed, it now launched cotton candy into the air like puffy rockets. The wall had fallen off the side of a brick two-story house beside it. The 10-foot-wide house had a cracked sign that read *Mega Mystery Mansion* in drippy red paint.

A woman with a slick gray bun and pointy nose walked into the cotton candy booth. She was hard to hear over the sound of the broken machine.

"What a disaster," she moaned. She pulled out her two-way radio. "Cotton candy shack near the entrance is down, Blue Bear. Add it to the repair list." She followed the candy machine's cord and unplugged it, ending the sugar cloud fun. "I'll get someone to make the announcement about the park closing early. If things keep breaking, we won't be able to open again for another month. Over." The woman tucked away her radio, nailed a closed sign to the Mega Mystery Mansion, and walked away.

A pang of sadness flowed through Ellie's

chest. Not because the mystery mansion was closed—they had a real mystery to solve now—but because she had promised Penny that she would fix this. And it sounded like they had very little time to solve this mystery. They had to get to work. Fast. But Fez, Tink, and Jessica were distracted by the games.

"Score!" Jessica yelled as her basketball swished into a flashing hoop.

Ellie decided to start looking for clues without them. Soon, she spotted six softball-sized holes in the ground and the collapsed wall.

She licked her sweet, sticky lips as she analyzed the wet yellow goo shimmering around the holes. She poked it, discovering it was sticky like maple syrup. And that wasn't her only discovery. At a fishing game shaped like a boat a few booths over, there was something sparkly sticking out of the wall.

She ran over and pulled a silky purple scarf out of the flower bed beside the fence. Normally, she would assume it was just a lost scarf. But it was sticky—just like the holes. She updated her suspect list.

Suspects

1. *Mystery person in hoodie – Breaking things. Why?*
2. *Mrs. Grinko – Threatened to shut down park*

Clues

1. *Sticky goop and holes in booths. Sabotage?*
2. *Scarf. Belongs to whoever is breaking things?*

As she scribbled the notes, a familiar peppery smell from the scarf tickled her nose. But before she could get a good whiff, someone tapped her on the shoulder. She quickly stuffed the evidence into her pocket.

"Hey, Ellie," said a familiar male voice. Ellie's eyes grew wide. She whirled toward the last person she wanted to deal with—Jack Grinko. Jack was always scaring Ellie and taunting her with the nickname Scaredy Bat. She didn't understand why he was always so mean to her. "Are you guys enjoying the park so far? This cotton candy explosion is something, eh?" he said with a fanged smile.

Ellie's eyebrow slammed together. Then, she opened her mouth, but no sound came out. She had never seen Jack be so polite. And she was pretty sure he had never called her by her real name before.

"It—it was definitely something," Ellie finally answered.

"Look, I'm sorry I've given you such a hard time. I feel bad that the Mega Mystery Mansion isn't open. I know you were looking forward to it. So, I got you a present," Jack said, holding out a can of Jelly Belly Monster Nuts. "Think of it as a peace offering. This is the new cherry flavor they came out with."

"Thanks," she said. Jack continued to smile at her, which made her stomach queasy. She thought she might puke before a flicker of movement caught her eye. The mystery person was weaving through the game booths nearby.

"Aren't you going to try them?" Jack asked. Wanting to get rid of him as fast as possible, Ellie opened the can without thinking.

BOING! An explosion of fake snakes sprang into her face.

"Eek!" Ellie screeched as she turned into a bat. *POOF!* She fled to the top of a ten-foot fishing pole with a fake fish the size of a monster tire hanging from it. Jack's laugh boomed from below.

"Once a Scaredy Bat, always a Scaredy Bat," he chirped before skipping away.

But Ellie didn't care about Jack's mean words—she had a bird's-eye view of the suspect.

Chapter Six

Batnapped

The hooded person was crouched by the red-and-yellow-striped ring-toss booth. They glanced left, then right before pulling a screwdriver out of their pocket. Holding it awkwardly in one hand, they twirled it against the booth's screws on the side.

Ellie scanned the rest of the park. She could tell the right side of the park had all the rides, with the game booths, Mega Mystery Mansion, and a few food shacks closer to the entrance. The left side was just a mishmash of color with an outdoor food court and lots of restaurants. Ellie spotted a truck with a pretzel and a mustard bottle painted on the side and began to drool.

A voice crackled on the loudspeaker. "Due

to some unexpected problems, Mega Adventureland will be closing in thirty minutes. We apologize for the inconvenience. All patrons will receive a ticket for a later date. We hope your day has been an adventure."

Ellie's heart sank. She squinted at the haunted house's clock tower on the far side of the park as it gonged loudly. That meant they only had until one o'clock before they got kicked out. Ellie turned back to the mystery person. *THUNK!* Just in time to see one of the ring-toss booth's walls fall.

Ellie gasped. This was evidence—the mystery person was taking things apart and breaking them. She needed to tell the rest of the mystery team. She flew to the ground to transform, but her tiny bat feet got stuck in the thick liquid by a hole. It may have felt only slightly sticky when she was big, but now it felt like superglue on her tiny bat feet. She tried to pull herself free by flying away. But no matter how hard she flapped, she wasn't getting any higher. She took deep breaths to calm herself and transform, but she couldn't. *This can't be happening again!* she thought.

She let out a loud squeak, hoping her friends would hear. What she didn't expect was to get the attention of the hooded person. They put down their tools to investigate the sound. Ellie's breathing became quick and shallow. The citrusy smell of oranges wafted toward her as the person got closer. Her head pounded like a drum. The mystery person reached into their hoodie pocket and silently pulled out a clear glass bottle. Ellie watched, trembling with wide eyes, as they bent down and squirted the cold, slippery liquid on her little bat paws. Whatever it was, it smelled fruity like strawberries. And most importantly, it got her feet unstuck.

"Ellie? Ellie? Where are you?" called Jessica.

Ellie shook like a leaf in a storm as the hooded figure's hand slowly drifted toward her. A white scar on their wrist bulged against the warm skin in a C shape.

"Squeak! Squeak!" Ellie yelled as she was lifted off the ground. Her heart was hammering against her chest like it was trying to escape.

"Ellie, where did you go?" called Tink.

The mystery person froze. *POOF!* And to Ellie's surprise, she turned back into a vampire—knocking over the mystery person. She stumbled backward into a bed of prickly red flowers. Once she scrambled back to her feet, the mystery person was gone. All that was left was the faint smell of oranges.

"There you are!" Jessica said, rushing around the corner with Fez and Tink.

Fez sniffed the air. "Mmm. Did you eat an

orange over here or something? Ellie, are you holding out on snacks?"

"Did you see them!?" Ellie asked, ignoring Fez.

"See who? Where did you even go?" Tink asked.

"The mystery person who almost kidnapped me!" Ellie said. She shoved the scarf into Tink's backpack as she spoke. She explained everything from not being able to control her transformation to fruity smells to the wrist scar.

"Woah! That sounds scary!" Jessica said when the story ended. She wrapped Ellie in a tight hug.

"It was," Ellie said.

"Here, maybe this will make you feel better," Fez said, holding a bat plushie in the palm of his hand. "I won it beating Jessica at the basketball game. You should have it. It reminds me of you."

Ellie took the soft bat and smiled. "Thanks, Fez."

"After we solve this mystery, I'm going to

win Jess a rat that looks just like her!"

Jessica groaned. "My rat eyes are not that red or beady when I transform."

Ellie couldn't help but giggle as she placed her new friend in her pocket. She turned to Tink, who was sitting quietly on a rock. He didn't say anything after she told her story, which was odd for him. Tink loved to give his theories.

"What do you think?" Ellie asked. Tink didn't answer. He was staring into the distance.

"Tink, are you okay?" Jessica asked.

"Yeah, you look like you were the one that almost got batnapped by the mystery person," Fez said.

"I doubt they were going to take Ellie," Tink said in a quiet, calm voice.

"You don't know that!" Ellie said. "You weren't there."

"No… But I know who the mystery person is."

Chapter Seven

Transformation Trouble

Tink pulled a photo out of his backpack. It was him and Lou at their favorite ice cream shop. They both were making goofy faces and giving the peace sign. And there, right on Lou's wrist, was the C-shaped scar.

"That's the scar!" Ellie exclaimed.

Tink groaned. "That's what I thought."

"No way!" squealed Jessica. "Why would Lou want to ruin the park?"

Tink frowned. "I don't think he would. But he has been acting weird lately. Maybe I just don't know him as well as I thought." He shook his head, crumpled the photo, and shoved it back into his bag.

"Maybe it's not what it seems," Fez said. "One time I was looking for frogs and I thought I caught one, but it ended up being a toad."

Jessica scrunched her nose. "They're pretty much the same."

"No way! A toad is bumpier and has shorter legs. Frogs have pointier noses and the way they hop is—hey, Tink, where are you going?"

"I just need a few minutes alone." He disappeared into a tall group of clowns walking toward the haunted house.

"Now what?" Jessica asked Ellie.

"I think we need to visit the scene of the crime. Let's go investigate where I saw Lou unscrew the wall." They went to the ring-toss booth, which now had all four walls.

"Ellie, are you sure you saw him unscrew the wall?" Fez asked, circling the booth. "Maybe you just thought it fell."

"Positive. I saw it, and I heard the bang it made." She ran her hand over the booth's smooth wooden wall. Nothing seemed out of place. There were no screws missing or holes. Her stomach sank. "What if Lou was fixing things, not breaking them?"

"But why hide in a hoodie if you're fixing things?" Jessica asked.

"I'm not sure," Ellie said. "I'm trying to trust my detective gut, though, and I don't feel like Lou would be hurting the park. At least not on purpose."

Fez's stomach grumbled. "My detective gut is telling me it is lunch time."

Ellie peered at the clock tower on the haunted house. "We only have fifteen minutes before the park closes," she said. "Let's try to figure out what these weird holes are before we're kicked out. Then we can get a snack. If we hurry, maybe we can get a mustard pretzel. They have a truck on the other side of the park."

Fez instantly snapped into action, looking for holes. "Found some!" he called from a booth with a wall of rainbow bears. He pointed to the side, where the plywood was spotted with jagged holes the size of grapefruits and golf balls.

"And look, there are holes in the ground too!" Ellie said.

"Maybe the park has rats," Fez said. "These holes look rat-sized, and rats like to chew through stuff AND burrow." He picked a fluffy flower from a nearby garden and twirled it in his fingers.

Jessica stifled a sneeze. "Fez, you need to stop waving that around. I'm going to sneeze, and you know what happens when I sneeze."

"Yeah. You turn into an adorable rat!" Fez exclaimed.

"Wait, that's a great idea!" Ellie said. "Turn into a rat, so we can compare any holes you make with these."

"What!?" Jessica cried. "You want me to turn into a rat and snack on some wood? No thanks. I prefer my food not to taste like tree bark."

"Actually, some types of gnome trees have bark that tastes like lemon pie!" Fez said. He held up the flower. "This is actually a Panisemo, and it tastes like fresh bread. At least, that's what it said in *Gnome Sweet Gnome: Cooking with Magic Plants.*"

"Come on, Jess," Ellie pleaded. "We're

running out of time. I promised Penny."

Jessica snatched the flower with a sigh.

Fez clapped. "I love this part!"

Jessica closed her eyes as she sniffed the flower. She opened one eye after a few deep inhales. "I can't do it if you're watching like that!" she said. "Turn around." Fez and Ellie did.

They turned around just in time to see the sun peeking out from a cloud. The light made something up on the hill beside the park glimmer. It was a pair of binoculars, and someone was watching them. It was far, but Ellie knew two things: the person was almost as tall as a tree. And they had wild green hair that stuck out like thick, wavy pipe cleaners.

"A-a-achoo!" Jessica sneezed, making Ellie jump. But to her surprise, she didn't turn into a bat, and Jessica didn't turn into a rat. Neither of them transformed.

"That's weird," Jessica said. "It always makes me transform." She tried again. "A-a-achoo!" But again, nothing happened. Whoever was on the hill was gone when Ellie looked back.

Thunder rumbled, and Jessica handed the flower back to Fez. "Sorry, I can't. This is giving me a major headache. Ugh, it feels like someone is pounding a drum in my brain."

Fez popped the flower in his mouth. "Woah! It really does taste like fresh bread."

"Maybe I can do the chew test," Ellie said. "Bats are kind of like flying rats." She tried to transform, but nothing happened. She clapped a hand over her throbbing forehead and gasped as she looked at Jessica. Her skin was starting to get faint blue spots. And Ellie knew that could only mean one thing. "I think something is draining our transformational powers."

"What does that mean?" Fez asked.

"That if we don't get away from whatever is draining us, we will continue to get sicker and sicker," Ellie explained. "Blue spots mean the power drain is really bad, and if it lasts too long, you can lose transformational powers forever."

Jessica's blue-spotted face turned a sickly green. "We need to get out of here. Now!"

Chapter Eight

Prime Suspect

The gang wove around crowds of people to reach the gate. But before they could get there, sheets of rain pounded down, making it almost impossible to see. Screams of people running for shelter echoed across the park, intermingling with low rumbles of thunder. Ellie wiped the water off her glasses, and a blurry outline of a bicycle-sized cup on a building appeared.

"This way!" she yelled over the rain and thunder. They yanked open a creaky wooden door and rushed into the sandy entrance. The water that poured off of them made the sand covering the floors into thick, squishy mud. The air smelled both earthy and fruity.

The beach-themed restaurant had a wood

bar lined with giant baskets of fruit. Behind it was a sky-blue wall with clouds and chunky glowing letters that read 'The Smoothie Shack.' There were also fake palm trees with trunks wrapped with rope and tables sheltered by straw umbrellas. And at one of those tables, on the other side of the room, sat Ava and Jack. Ava pulled out a purple pencil from her bag and sketched in a heart-covered notebook.

"We could be having fun right now if you didn't mess up," Jack snarled at Ava.

"I can't control the rain," Ava said, switching

to another color.

"You know that's not what I meant. We wouldn't still be in Brookside right now if you didn't mess up your job. Mom and Grandma are right—you've changed." He got up and slammed his chair into the table before walking out the back door. Ava sat in silence, staring at the pencil in her hand. Ellie had disliked Jack before, but watching him make Ava sad made her not like him even more. She forgot that they should be trying to leave the park and went to comfort her friend.

"Are you okay?" Ellie asked.

Ava sprang up from her chair with wide eyes. "Sweet pudding! You scared me… how long have you been standing there?"

"Long enough," Jessica chimed in. "What did Jack mean when he said you wouldn't be in Brookside if you didn't mess up?" As they drew closer, what Ava was working on became clear: a drawing of the smoothie bar.

Ava stared down at the sand and shuffled her feet. "Oh, um, I had this job at an ice cream shop. And my parents said if I did well, Jack and I could go to Typhoon's Terror Park a few towns over. But I got fired. Jack was super mad because he loves Typhoon. When we were younger, he even tried to grow out his hair, dye it green, and braid it. He thought it would look like Typhoon's giant head snakes."

"Why?" asked Ellie.

"I guess he thought Typhoon's green snake hair looked good," Ava said.

"No, why did you get fired?" Ellie said.

Before Ava could answer, a sopping wet and panting Tink burst through the door. Ellie, Fez, and Jessica all whirled around to face him—blocking Ava from view.

"Woah, you look out of breath. You okay?" Fez asked.

Tink rested his hands on his knees. "Yes, but holy moly, that's a lot of rain. I'm so glad you guys are here, because I figured something out. I opened my backpack for some water and the whole bag smelled like girl. It turns out it was the scarf you found. And it smells exactly like Mrs. Grinko's stinky perfume."

"Um, Tink," Jessica said.

"That means the scarf probably belongs to her!" Tink continued. "If she is behind this, then Lou probably has nothing to do with it. And let's be honest, that whole Grinko family is pretty much trouble. Well, except Ava. She's just pretty."

"Tink, you might want to—" Ellie said, but Tink kept going.

"So if Mrs. Grinko is behind this mystery, Lou could have been sneaking around for another reason. Maybe he was just testing his invisibility formula. He obviously has it with him. That's why he smelled like oranges. Either way, Mrs. Grinko should be our prime suspect!"

Ellie, Jessica, and Fez stepped aside to reveal Ava sitting behind them.

Tink's eyes bulged, and he gave an awkward wave. "Oh, hi, Ava."

Chapter Nine
Warning

"Why is my mom a prime suspect?" Ava asked. The only sound was the rain pounding on the roof of The Smoothie Shack. "Is anyone going to answer me? Why is my mom's scarf evidence? And how did you even get it?"

"One second," Ellie said. She turned toward Jessica, Tink, and Fez. "Should we trust her?" she whispered.

"I can hear you," Ava whispered back. Ellie blushed. After everyone agreed, Ellie explained all the strange things happening in the park.

"Is that why my head feels like it's going to explode?" Ava asked. "I thought it was just from Jack." Ava stood up. "If something is draining our powers, we need to get out of here ASAP." She ran to the front door, but the rain continued to pour down in sheets. Just as soon as she opened it, she slammed it shut. "Oh, this isn't good," she said. "I need to find my mom and Jack."

Jessica crossed her arms over her chest. "You sure you just aren't covering for your mom?"

Ava chewed her lip. "I can tell you for sure my mom has nothing to do with this. I don't know why that scarf was by the game booth. She left it in the car before we got into the park, which was right before we saw you. Didn't you notice she wasn't wearing a scarf? And wasn't stuff breaking down long before we all got here?"

"Maybe she came earlier to sabotage some stuff?" Tink suggested.

Ava dug in a sequin purse and pulled out a photo strip with four frames. "I have proof!" she said. Each photo had Jack, Ava, and their mother making funny faces. Well, mostly Jack and Ava. More importantly, it had the date

and time the photo was taken— 11:30 that day—which lined up with Ava's story.

Ellie answered first. "No, that wouldn't make sense, because she is wearing the scarf in these photos. She would have lost it while sabotaging." She handed Ava the scarf, then updated her list. Thinking about what Ava had said about Typhoon owning a park nearby, she added him as a suspect—he looked just like whoever was spying on the hill.

Suspects

1. ~~Mystery person in hoodie – Breaking things. Why? Lou~~
2. ~~Mrs. Grinko – Threatened to shut down park~~
3. *Typhoon spying on hill. Sabotaging park so he has less competition?*

Clues

1. *Sticky goop and holes in booths. Sabotage?*
2. ~~Scarf. Belongs to whoever is breaking things?~~
3. *Something draining vampire powers*

Jessica sat at a table with her head down. "Fez, that blender is not helping my headache!"

"Sorry, just a second longer," Fez shouted over the whirling machine. He stood behind the counter with a blender full of pink, swirling liquid. "I heard that strawberry banana smoothies are good for vampire headaches."

Jessica stuck out her tongue. "Count me

out. Strawberries are gross." She turned to Ellie. "So Typhoon is now our only suspect?"

"Yes, and when the rain slows down, we should go interrogate him. It actually sounds like it is only drizzling now."

Jessica cocked her head to the side. Ellie followed her gaze and watched as Ava picked up a piece of paper sitting on top of the sand beside the entrance. The blender finally stopped. Ava's hand shook as she read the note out loud.

"Get out of the park now! Before it's too late!"

Chapter Ten

Mega Mystery Mansion

Ellie, Tink, Jessica, and Ava ran outside, looking for the mysterious note writer. They circled The Smoothie Shack, but there was no one anywhere. The whole amusement park was eerily quiet. Especially since the rain had slowed to a drizzle. Even the hill where Typhoon was spying earlier was now empty.

"I don't see anyone," Ellie said. "Did you see the note slide under the door?"

"No," said Ava. "I just noticed it sitting there. Who knows how long it was there for?"

"So for all we know, Ava could have planted it," Jessica said.

Ava handed the note to Ellie. "No way! Why would I?"

Jessica massaged her throbbing head. "I

don't know. This headache is making me loopy. Sorry."

Ellie scanned the note. It was pretty plain, but the writing was smudged.

"Wait, Hailey Haddie's book on how to be a detective says that left-handed people often smudge ink when they write. Someone left-handed wrote this," Ellie said. She glanced at Ava's left hand in the pink sling, which ruled her out. Even though Ellie didn't ask, Ava also insisted on showing her good hand to prove it was free of ink smudges. As Ellie did so, her eyes fell to the muddy footprints on the step of The Smoothie Shack where Ava was standing. They weren't shoe prints, but actual tiny footprints. The rain was slowly washing them away. Before she could get a closer look, Fez came racing out of The Smoothie Shack with two cups.

"These should help your heads," he said as he passed the fruity drinks to Ellie and Ava. "Where is everyone? It's so quiet now."

Jessica rubbed her arms. "I know. Kind of creepy. Let's get out of here."

Ava glanced around the empty park. "Maybe my mom and brother are already at the car." The girls slurped down their smoothies as they made their way to the front gate.

"Are you sure you don't want some?" Ava asked. "It seems to help."

Jessica stuck out her tongue. "Yuck. No thank you. I hate strawberries." They walked past the merry-go-round, which was empty but still spinning to a happy tune. Relief flooded Ellie's body when the gate came into sight, but it didn't last long.

"The gate is locked!" Jessica cried. "This can't be happening!" She frantically tugged on the bars and tried to slip through the gaps. Next, she tried to climb the fence, but it was over twice her height.

"Did the park close and they forgot about us?" Ava asked.

"I don't think so," Tink answered. "The parking lot is still filled with cars. There is something mega strange going on at Mega Adventureland." A bush beside a nearby flower bed rustled.

Ellie put her finger over her lips. "Shh," she whispered. They watched as the bush once again shook.

"Someone go investigate," Ellie whispered.

"Why can't you go?" Tink asked.

Ellie shrugged. "Um, well, I guess I could—"

"Ava! Ava!" yelled Jack from the merry-go-round. "Mom is in trouble!" He stopped in front of the group, wide-eyed and panting.

"What!?" Ava cried. "Is this a trick? You better not be joking."

Jack wiped a tear streaming down his cheek. "I'm not! I saw her get pulled into the haunted house with some sort of green rope. I don't know what is going on, but I'm scared, and my head is pounding. We need to find Mom and get out of here."

"We can help," Ellie said. She expected a mean comment about how a Scaredy Bat couldn't help. But Jack agreed.

"Then let's go!" he said, taking off at a sprint, leading the way.

They ran toward the haunted house that looked like a mini mansion. Even though it was the size of a classroom, it was three times as tall. It had fake ghosts flying out the clock tower's windows and red eyes glowing in the holes between the crumbling bricks. From the bottom of the house, giant green roots snaked in and out of the cracks before tangling with the vines strangling the chimney. The steps up to the door were flooded with sticky liquid. Muffled screams echoed from behind the metal front door.

Ellie gulped. "Maybe those are just ride sound effects."

"Ava! Jack! Get me out of here!" bellowed a voice inside.

"Mom!" Jack and Ava both said in unison. All six kids tugged at the sticky front door, but it wouldn't budge. It was covered in the same holes they had seen on the game booth, along with the sticky substance.

Jack pounded on the door. "Mom! Mom!" he yelled. "I'm coming." After a few seconds of ramming the door, he slunk to the ground and cradled his head in his hands. "Ow!"

"Jack? What's wrong?" Ava asked. The bell

MEGA MYSTERY
MANSION

on the clock tower chimed loudly across the park. It was 1:30.

"My head hurts. A lot," Jack said in a low voice. "That bell isn't helping." Ava shook her smoothie, but it was empty. Ellie opened her cup, but it was empty too.

"We need more smoothie!" shouted Ava. Jessica slunk down on the ground beside Jack, her eyes barely open. Ellie bent down to try to talk to Jessica, but she was passed out.

"Jess? Jess?" Ellie said. She gave her friend a gentle shake. "Jessica. Wake up!" Ellie's heart was beating so hard, it felt like it was going to burst through her chest.

"We need to split up," Ava said. "Ellie and I will go grab the smoothies. Tink and Fez, stay here with these two." Both boys agreed. Ellie took one last look at Jack and Jessica, leaning lifelessly against the haunted house. She wiped away tears as she dashed back to The Smoothie Shack with Ava.

Chapter Eleven

When You Feel Lost

Ellie's hands shook as she plunked a banana into the blender. A couple hours ago, she'd only had a gut feeling that this was a mystery. And now this was the most intense case she and the gang had ever worked on. Ava threw strawberries and water into the blender and flicked it on.

As the thick, pink liquid swirled around the blender, thoughts of poor Jessica and Jack whirled around Ellie's head.

"If they lose their transformational powers, it isn't the end of the world," Ellie said. She meant to say it just to herself for a bit of comfort, but her brain felt like a scrambled egg. She ended up saying it out loud.

"You don't understand," said Ava. "In my

family, that might be one of the worst things. Jack and I aren't allowed to transform into our animals, except during our weekend transformation practices. Mom always said we need to hide them. She's super afraid humans will turn on vampires again and we will have to go into hiding."

Ellie poured the smoothies into cups. "That sounds stressful. Your family seems… intense."

Ava groaned. "You don't know the half of it—OH MY GOODNESS!" Ava jumped up on the bar. "Snake!" she screeched, pointing to the sandy floor with a trembling finger. "A giant green snake!" Ellie jumped on the bar with Ava. She was terrified of snakes. To her relief, there was no snake when she looked at the sandy ground. But there were long, snaky drag marks.

BANG! Fez and Tink crashed through the door. "They vanished!" Tink cried. "Jessica and Jack disappeared."

"What? How? You were supposed to be watching them!" Ava exclaimed.

"We were. They just disappeared into thin air. Like they faded," Fez said.

"Is it some sort of weird vampire thing?" Tink asked. "Us humans definitely don't just fade into nothing like that."

"*You humans* let my brother disappear!" Ava snarled. She jumped off the bar and bolted out the door. "Jack! Jack!" she yelled, her voice becoming fainter every second. Ellie's face turned a ghostly white, and she froze.

"Did you hear us?" Fez asked after a few moments.

"Jessica is gone?" Ellie asked. Tink and Fez nodded. Ellie took off running, and the boys followed.

The haunted house was quiet by the time she got there. No more sounds came from inside. And she didn't see Ava. The only noise was a bush rustling, but when Ellie checked it, no one was there.

"I think we need to call for help," Tink said. Ellie agreed, but they realized none of them had a phone. And the only way out of the park was locked.

"Okay, plan B," Tink said. "We solve this mystery."

Ellie shook her head. "I don't think even

Hailey Haddie could solve this mystery. And she's the best detective ever. It's pointless."

"It's not pointless," Tink said. "If we can figure it out, we can find Jessica and Jack. Then we can get out of here."

"I don't think telling her we're going to find Jack is the way to go," Fez whispered.

Ellie pulled out her notebook and flipped through her notes. She read through the filled-out pages from the other mysteries the team had solved: the frozen vampires, the sunscreen snatcher, the missing jellyfish, and the haunted movie set.

Finally, she spoke. "You're right. We need to do this. I am not losing one of my best friends over this."

"That's the spirit!" said Fez. "But where do we start?"

"When a mystery makes you feel lost, go back to your notes. At least, that's what Hailey Haddie always says in her show," Tink said.

Ellie nodded. She grabbed her notebook and updated it with a shaky hand.

Suspects

1. ~~*Mystery person in hoodie – Breaking things. Why? Lou*~~
2. ~~*Mrs. Grinko – Threatened to shut down park*~~
3. *Typhoon spying on hill. Sabotaging park so he has less competition?*

Clues

1. *Sticky goop and holes in booths. Sabotage?*
2. ~~*Scarf. Belongs to whoever is breaking things?*~~
3. *Something draining vampire powers*
4. *Jessica and Jack disappearing*
5. *Snake tracks?*

After they couldn't find Ava, the trio headed back to The Smoothie Shack to take a look at the snake tracks. Ellie analyzed the slither marks in the sand with her magnifying glass. They led to the left side of the restaurant and circled back out a hole behind a jukebox.

Ellie paced the room, trying to figure out

why the snake would come in there. She stopped and stared at Ava's drawing of the smoothie bar for a few seconds. It sure was realistic. She had gotten the placement of the blenders and fruit just right. The baskets of bananas, pineapples, apples, and mangoes. But what was the purple pile of fruit on the left side? That wasn't there in real life.

"Come look at this," Ellie said. "Did Ava just add a basket of purple fruit?"

"Wait, there used to be lots of purple fruit

in here, like plums and grapes," Fez said. "I know because I thought, 'who puts those in a smoothie?'"

"That's what the snake must have come in here for!" Ellie said.

"Okay, but what kind of snake likes fruit? Particularly purple fruit?" Tink asked.

"Jack said he saw his mom being dragged into the haunted house by a green rope. And Ava said she saw a green snake slithering in The Smoothie Shack. What if they're the same thing? And I only know one person that has giant green snakes—we need to try to find Typhoon."

"From his commercials, I know he's really big. Like as tall as a tree. So how would he sneak around the park?" Fez asked.

"Hmm, he would be pretty big to sneak around and break things… But nothing says he didn't have help from some snakes," Ellie said. "I bet if we follow those tracks, we will find Typhoon and his snakes!"

Chapter Twelve
Disappearing Act

The snake tracks outside had the same sticky, yellow liquid they'd found earlier, making them easy to follow on the pavement. They wove through the park, all the way to the mermaid fountain, before disappearing.

"Looks like a dead end," Tink said. "No Typhoon or snakes."

"Maybe not," Ellie said. "But this fountain was full of water earlier. I know because the cotton candy was melting in it when we first got in. So how could all that water be gone now? It even rained. If anything, it should be extra full."

Fez circled the fountain. "I don't see any holes for the water to leak out, but there are holes in the ground over here. Just like we found at the booths."

Ellie tapped her finger on her lip. "I bet Typhoon got his snakes to drink all the water. He is known to set fires, and water would only get in the way. So he got his snakes to travel underground and do the dirty work and break things. Maybe after the park was closed, he planned on coming inside to ruin the rest with fire!"

"It sort of makes sense, but most snakes don't burrow underground," Fez said.

"And that doesn't explain why Jessica and Jack disappeared, and what is causing the vampire power drain," Tink said.

Ellie felt silly. "Sorry, I should have made sure it made sense before saying it out loud," she said.

"I like when you tell us your theories out loud," Fez said. "It helps me think!"

"Same here," Tink said. "What is making those holes? Is it related to the sticky substance we keep running into? How is Typhoon doing all of this?"

"I don't think he is," Ava said. The three

startled friends turned to see Ava standing nearby with red, puffy eyes.

"Ava! Where were you?" Fez asked.

Ava dabbed her teary eye. "Looking for my mom and Jack. But there was no one at the haunted house anymore. At least, no people screaming inside. I heard a whispering sound and found a little girl with red pigtails behind the house. But she ran away as soon as she saw me. I think maybe she lost her parents or something. I tried to chase her, but geez, for someone half my height, she was twice as fast."

"That's odd," Tink said. "In the rain earlier, I also thought I saw a little girl with pigtails."

"Maybe she is working with Typhoon to sabotage the park," Ellie offered. "It feels like we're getting close to finding him."

Ava shook her head. "But Typhoon can't be behind this. Like I said earlier, Jack is obsessed with him. So that means I know way more than I ever wanted to about the guy. Typhoon and his snakes are allergic to Clovertine flowers." She motioned toward the flower beds blanketed in orange four-leaf clovers with spiky centers. "There are tons of them around here, so there is no way they would come into the park. And he doesn't trust anyone else to do his dirty work. Jack applied to be his assistant one summer and was laughed out of the office."

"That's some really good detective work," Tink said.

A pang of jealously ached in Ellie's stomach. "Are you sure?" she asked.

"Positive," Ava said. "I know Clovertine flowers when I see them. I used to be obsessed with drawing Gnome plants and using them to make perfume." Ellie crossed Typhoon off her list.

Suspects

1. ~~*Mystery person in hoodie – Breaking things. Why? Lou*~~
2. ~~*Mrs. Grinko – Threatened to shut down park*~~
3. ~~*Typhoon spying on hill. Sabotaging park so he has less competition?*~~

Clues

1. *Sticky goop and holes in booths. Sabotage?*
2. ~~*Scarf. Belongs to whoever is breaking things?*~~
3. *Something draining vampire powers*
4. *Jessica and Jack disappearing*
5. *Snake tracks?*

Ellie groaned. "That means we are out of suspects."

Fez picked a green orb-shaped flower beside the Clovertine. "Aren't gnome plants super cool? It's crazy that only gnomes know how to grow Clovertine flowers and all these other rare plants. That's why most of them become gardeners." He pulled the tattered book of gnome plants from Tink's backpack.

"They are really cool," Ava agreed. "But dangerous if you don't know your plants. I made Jack try my homemade perfume made from Flavell flower sap once, and he ended up in the hospital. My parents were so mad. It turns out that it can drain vampire powers." She sighed heavily. "I hope wherever Jack is that he's okay."

"Wait, what?" Ellie said.

"I hope he's okay," Ava repeated. "I know you two don't get along, but—"

"No, about the sap draining powers," Ellie said.

"Is there a type of plant sap that can make someone disappear?" Tink asked.

"Sort of. It can slowly digest you and teleport you into a plant's stomach," Fez said.

"Oh good, then I know where I'm going," Tink said, his breathing fast and heavy.

Ellie gasped. Tink's colors were fading, and his body was becoming see-through. He was disappearing.

"Fez, how do we stop this?" Ellie asked, grabbing Tink's arm. "Tink, are you okay?"

"Yeah, just light and tingly," Tink answered. Fez frantically flipped through the book, but it wasn't long before Ellie could see through his whole body too. The book dropped to the ground with a thump.

"Uh oh. This really is tingly," Fez said with a giggle. "It kind of tickles."

Ava dove to try to grab Fez, but it was no use. Tink and Fez dissolved from their hands like cotton candy in water. The two girls were alone.

Chapter Thirteen

Blumungous

"This can't be happening!" Ellie shrieked. She and Ava frantically waved their arms where Tink and Fez had just stood. But now, there was nothing but the chilly autumn air.

"First Jessica and Jack, and now Tink and Fez. Are we next?" Ellie cried. She held her hands in front of her, turning them over repeatedly. She'd wanted to save the park for Penny's birthday party, but now she had to solve this mystery to get her friends back.

Ellie buttoned up her trench coat, suddenly feeling like a popsicle.

She picked up the plant book and handed it to Ava. "Try to find what kind of plant could have done this." Ava leaned the book against her pink sling as she flipped through pages. Ellie analyzed the ground, looking for any clues as to where the boys disappeared.

"Ellie, I don't know what I'm looking for," Ava said. "There are hundreds of gnome plants."

"Look for anything with snake tracks, a green snake, missing water. Um, people disappearing. Sticky liquid. Power draining. Oh! Fez said something about a plant digesting you and teleporting you?" The page flipping stopped.

Ava paused, and her mouth fell open. "No way. It can't be. This plant is super rare, but it sure sounds right." Ellie looked at the page with a torn top corner. It had a picture of a blue daisy with one round eye in the center. Its tangle of roots oozed yellow sap. It sat beside a regular daisy and was almost three times as tall.

Blumungous Flower

A rare flower that belongs to the daisy family. It has been banned in most countries due to its watering needs, stealing habit, hazardous sap, and bad listening.

Water: This plant requires tons of water. Full-sized Blumungous' roots will travel underground and suck dry entire lakes.

Stealing: Each plant will steal things to gift to the gnome that grew it. It can't resist items that are the gnome's favorite color.

Sap: The sticky sap from the plant roots is known to cause vampire headaches and drain powers. This sap will eventually cause those who touch it to teleport into the plant's stomach. At that time, they will be fully digested if not freed within the hour.

Bad listening: Will only listen to the commands of the gnome that grew it.

Notes: Put strawberries into the plant's mouth to make it spit out anything in its stomach. Vampires that eat strawberries will also slow down the sap power drain and plant stomach teleportation.

Ellie flipped the page over, but there was nothing else about Blumungous flowers. The ripped corner should have included the plant size. Luckily, there was a Blumungous photo, and from that she estimated it was about as tall as a sitting cat.

"Okay, okay," Ava said, taking a deep breath. "We just need to get them out before they've been in there an hour. The only problem is, I have no idea when Jessica and Jack disappeared."

"I do," Ellie said. "The big clock tower had just struck 1:30. It's 2:00 now, so we have half an hour to get some magic plant to spit up."

"If we don't disappear first," Ava said. "I haven't even seen that daisy plant. If we don't know where it is, how are we going to make it give our friends back?"

"We are going to lure it with the color it steals the most," Ellie said.

Ava scanned the book page. "But we don't know that."

"Yes, we do. Come on!"

Chapter Fourteen

One Way Or Another

Ellie and Ava burst into The Smoothie Shack. They gobbled down handfuls of strawberries as they stuffed their pockets full of the red fruit. Then, they rubbed leftover smoothie on themselves for extra protection.

"I'll get the rope. You get the empty basket," Ellie instructed. She unwound the trunk of one of the fake palm trees.

"I think we should set the trap at the haunted house," Ava said, dumping out a banana basket. "When I was looking for Jack, I noticed that the haunted house had a ton of sap around it. So I think the flower has been spending a lot of time there."

Ellie paused. "You're right. There was a lot of sap there. How could one small flower make that much? Do you think there is more than one Blumungous?"

Ava's shoulders slumped. "If there is, how will we know which one to feed the strawberries?!"

"Hold on, where is that book? I have an idea!" Ellie declared. "We may not have to catch the plant if we can catch the gnome that grew it. Gnomes can talk to their plants, so we can figure out which one did it."

Ava handed Ellie the book. "How do you know if the gnome is even around here?" Ava asked.

Ellie told her about the gardener at the gate and the tiny footprints she had seen outside after they found the warning note by the door.

"I should have realized a gnome probably left those wet footprints sooner," Ellie said. She flipped to the page on gnomes. "But in our rush to leave the park, I completely forgot about them. Until now. Who else would walk barefoot in this rainy cold? Gnomes don't even like to wear shoes in the snow. What if a gnome knew their plant was dangerous and was warning us? I can explain more later."

Ava agreed. "Later, I also need to tell you something." Ellie nodded, only half paying attention.

"I got it!" Ellie said, tapping the book page. "It says that a gnome's favorite food is mustard. They can't resist it. And I know where we can get some. Follow me!"

The two girls wove through the game booths and into the outdoor food court called *Adventure Eats*. Chairs and tables were lined up on the tiled cement, with a giant piece of glass corn in the middle. The clear cob was twice the height of Ellie, with bits of blue lightning whizzing around inside. After snaking around a nacho stand and a hotdog vendor, they spotted the food truck with a painted pretzel and mustard bottle on the side.

"Score!" Ava said, opening a vat of mustard inside. A tangy, vinegar smell filled the truck. They grabbed a bowl and scooped up a glob of the creamy, yellow condiment. Finally, they were ready to set their trap. They raced back to the creepy house as fast as their feet would take them.

They tied one end of the rope to the basket and threw it over the low branch of a nearby tree. Then, once they pulled the basket up with the rope, they set the mustard underneath. Their trap was set. Both Ellie and Ava held the rope as they peered through the dripping bush leaves.

"As soon as the gnome grabs the mustard, we will let go of the rope," Ellie whispered. Ava nodded. The clock read 2:15, meaning they only had fifteen minutes.

The sky was still a dark gray, but the rain clouds had passed. Ellie kept her eyes glued to the basket. Every now and then, a swirl of crunchy leaves would breeze by, but no gnome. The clock struck 2:20. Only ten minutes left.

Ava chewed her bottom lip. "We're running out of time," she whispered. "What is Plan B?" Ellie's breath caught in her throat. She'd thought this plan was so good that she didn't think of another. Just as she was about to tell Ava that, a loud whisper came from behind the haunted house.

"Do you hear that?" Ava asked. Ellie nodded. The two girls tiptoed around clumps of crunchy leaves to investigate. Against the back wall of the haunted house was a short girl with red braids and a green dress talking to the house. She held a single strawberry in her hand.

"That's the little girl I saw earlier," Ava whispered.

"What do you mean you won't eat it?" she asked. "You have to do what I say—I planted you."

A low mumble came from the house.

"That's not a little girl—that's a gnome," Ellie whispered. She pointed to the star mark on her arm—something all gnomes were born with. "She must be talking to the Blumungous." She squinted at the grass around the house, but she didn't see any flowers.

"Please just eat the strawberry," the gnome said. "I told you not to digest those people. You have to spit them out. They're running out of time."

Anger bubbled in Ellie's stomach. Those

people were her friends. She started smooshing the strawberries in her pocket between her fists.

"Follow my lead," she said to Ava. "We're getting that plant to eat strawberries one way or another. One, two, three."

Ellie dashed out of the bush with a fistful of drippy strawberry mush. She raced toward the gnome, her battle cry echoing over the wind. Ava followed. Both girls shot strawberries where the gnome was looking. The gnome let out a piercing scream.

Ellie dove to the ground, ready to stuff strawberries in the flowers' mouths. The problem was, there were no flowers. There was only grass and leaves.

"Where is it?" Ava said. "Where is the Blumungous?" A thick, green snake poked its head out from under the house. With a scream, Ellie threw a strawberry at it as she stumbled backward onto the grass.

"No, wait!" cried the gnome. "It hates getting strawberry juice on its roots!" But it was too late.

A deafening, dinosaur-like roar exploded from inside the house. The walls and ground cracked as they vibrated. The roof blasted off like a rocket, and a blue petal the size of a car poked out, followed by several more. In the seedy center was a beady eye glaring at the vampires. The bottom of the center was missing seeds. Instead, it had red lips twisted into a fangy frown.

"It DID NOT look this big in the book," Ava said, slowly backing away. Ellie glanced around for the gnome, but she was gone.

Chapter Fifteen

Speed Monkey Monster Coaster

The Blumungous flower let out a cry that shook the ground once more. The blue, humongous flower was bigger—and angrier—than Ellie had ever imagined. She patted her pockets for something to use against the angry flower. All she had was her notebook, Monster Spray, the sticky bat plushie, and mushy strawberries. A green root snaked toward Ellie, swiping at her foot. She didn't want to waste strawberries on roots, so she gave it a spritz with her Monster Spray. The fall air filled with a lavender scent, but nothing else happened. The thick root continued trying to grab her legs.

She ran the other way, joining Ava. They both turned around and tried to throw strawberries at its head, but it was too high. The girls dove into a bush to hide. Ellie peeked through the leaves at the clock—they only had five minutes to try to get strawberries into the monster flower's mouth. Or else their friends might be gone forever.

"Ellie, I have an idea," Ava whispered. "Look how high that roller coaster goes. If we can get it working, you'll be high enough to get the strawberries right into that flower's mouth. It would be such a short throw. I can make sure it opens its mouth at exactly the right time by putting strawberry on its roots again."

Ellie's palms were so sweaty, she wondered if she could even hold a strawberry at this point. She craned her neck to see the top of the coaster. The tallest peak disappeared into the gray sky, giving her a lump in her throat. "It's a good idea," Ellie said, trying to swallow the lump. "But you have to ride the coaster. I'm afraid of heights."

"I can't," Ava said. "My good arm can't throw anything right now." She held up her pink sling. "Ellie, it has to be you. Time is running out."

Tears stung Ellie's eyes as she glanced at the ticking tower clock. She knew Ava was right.

"Let's go," Ellie said. The girls ran toward the sign that read *Speed Monkey Monster Coaster*. Ellie jumped into a roller coaster cart with flaming bananas on the side. She tried to calm herself down with deep breathing, but it wasn't helping. She was about to go higher than she had ever been, and she couldn't even turn into a bat to get down. Nausea flooded her stomach as it churned with fear.

"Are you ready?" Ava asked, standing at the control panel.

Ellie checked her seatbelt and the bar with a shaky hand. "Ready." Ava pushed the glowing green button. The coaster jerked forward.

"When I see the roller coaster coming down the hill, I'll strawberry the roots," she said. "Good luck!"

The roller coaster climbed the steep hill, thumping every few feet. Soon, Ellie had a perfect view of the clock. Only two minutes. Which meant there was only one chance for this ride. She clenched her eyes shut, trying to think what Hailey Haddie would do. But the darkness just made her stomach churn more.

"Okay, eyes open," Ellie said to herself. She squeezed the strawberries in her pocket. "It's okay. You've got this." She peeked over the edge of the climbing coaster cart. Ava was the size of a grape. Ellie whipped her head back up, deciding that looking down was not the way to go. It wasn't long before only a thick grayness surrounded her. The only clear shapes were the roller coaster and herself. Everything else was swallowed by a thick, frosty fog. Then, with a *SQUEAK*! and a *TUNK!*, the roller coaster jerked to a stop.

"Please don't be stuck. Please don't be stuck," Ellie begged. Her hand, which clenched the strawberries, trembled extra hard. *TUNK!* The coaster started again, shifting Ellie's weight forward. The coaster slowly crawled across the top of the hump before falling like a bowling ball.

“Ahh!” Ellie screamed. The coaster rocketed down the hill, and the Blumungous came into view. The giant flower’s roar shook the roller coaster, and Ellie knew this was her chance. She threw the strawberries with all her strength. But the flower was almost ten car widths away—much farther than she’d thought it would be. And although she smacked its eye and head, she couldn’t hit its mouth. At the bottom of the hill, she zipped through a loop-de-loop. The strawberries, monster spray, notepad, and bat plushie dumped out of her pockets. Ellie scrambled to grab a falling strawberry but instead ended up with the bat.

"Noooo!" she shrieked. She didn't need a bat. She needed strawberries. The roller coaster rocketed up another hill as Ellie started to cry. She looked at the bat through bleary eyes, thinking about her friends. She stuffed the bat in her strawberry pocket without thinking. The soft body slurped up the remaining juice like a mop. Thinking she had just ruined the last thing Fez gave her, anger jolted through her body. But it wasn't long before it was replaced with hope.

She pulled the bat out of her pocket. This was her last chance. And the closest she would get to the flower's head—only three car widths away. If she could get the strawberry-soaked stuffed animal into the plant's mouth, it might be enough. The roller coaster zipped around a double loop that surrounded the haunted house. Ellie pulled her arm back just as the plant let out another deafening c-ry.

"Three, two, one!" she counted.

Chapter Sixteen

Nothing Exciting Happens in Brookside

The bat launched through the air—right into the flower's mouth. The Blumungous gulped it down and quickly started to heave. Its head bobbed back and forth as it made a sound like a cat passing a hairball. Then, in a gush of green goo, a group of people slid down its long pink tongue onto the ground. The plant panted for breath as it hung its head.

Ellie's wild roller coaster finally stopped. She jumped out of the cart and ran to the mess of people. Jessica, Tink, and Fez were there, covered in the green goo.

"You're okay!" Ellie squealed. She hugged

her gooey friends as tight as she could.

"Ick, what happened?" Jessica asked.

Ava wove through the gooey people. "Jack? Mom?" she called, but there were no other Grinkos in sight. After another minute of searching, Ava collapsed on the ground. "They're… they're gone," she whimpered.

A loud gagging sound came from the plant once more. And to Ava's delight, her family slid out. Mrs. Grinko sprang to her feet instantly and tried to shake off the goo. Ava slid over to hug her brother.

"Ava, you're okay!" Jack said, squeezing his slimy sister.

"I am suing!" Mrs. Grinko screamed. "Sueing. Unbelievable. Jack, Ava, let's go."

"Mom, you were just spit up by a plant. Don't you want to sit down for a second?" Ava asked.

"Ava, I want a lot of things. With a hot bath being at the top of that list right now. But no, I don't want to sit down. Let's. Go." She stomped away. Jack and Ava looked at each other, sighed, and then followed their mother.

A piercing scream came from the flower, and the ground shook like an earthquake. Roots burst from the soil, wrapping around anyone close by.

"We need the gnome," Fez said. "Only they can tell it to stop." Ellie looked around frantically for the gnome. She finally spotted her running away with the bowl of mustard.

"Oh, no, you don't," Ellie said. She sprinted after the gnome and tackled her to the ground. "Make your flower stop," she demanded.

The gnome started breathing heavy and fast. "I can't. I'm—I'm sorry, I've lost control. There is nothing I can do. Now please, please let me go."

"Try," Ellie commanded. The shaking ground was cracking. "Hurry!"

The gnome took a deep breath. "Please stop," she said in a meek voice.

"Louder!" Jessica said.

"Blue, stop!" the gnome said louder. The plant continued to flail its roots angrily.

"Louder!" said all four friends at once. The gnome inhaled deeply and yelled "Stop!" so loud that the mystery team thought their eardrums were going to pop. The flower's roots became still. Then, the Blumungous slunk back down into the haunted house. But not before spitting out one last person—Lou landed on the grass with a soft thud. His frizzy gray hair was everywhere, and his glasses were smudged with goo.

"Alma, I have the best idea for a new ride!" he said to the woman with the gray bun. The same one Ellie had seen at the cotton candy shack earlier.

"Lou Bear!" she said, hugging him. Ellie realized that she must have been talking to Lou on the radio.

"Lou Bear?" Tink said.

Lou turned to Tink and gave a small smile and wave. "Oh, um. That's just my code name. I was helping Alma fix the park."

Alma laughed. "Lou, people are going to find out we were dating eventually. I know it's still new, but what better time than after a plant throws you up?"

Lou laughed, and Tink smiled. "I left you guys a note," Lou said. "I tried to help the gnome gardener's daughter, Vienna, by building the haunted house around the plant. But it just kept getting bigger. By the time I realized what kind of plant it was, I was fading. So I made her promise to give you the note to get out of the park. I wanted Tink and all his friends to be safe."

Tink ran and hugged Lou. "I'm glad you're okay. And I'm glad you're not scared to talk to girls anymore."

Lou turned bright red as he wrapped his arms around Tink. "Shh. No one needed to know about that."

"So this whole thing was an accident?" Ellie asked Vienna.

The little gnome hung her head. "Not exactly. My family moved to Brookside after my dad got a job here. I've been helping him with the landscaping, but secretly growing Blue. I knew the flower would cause vampires to get headaches. I thought that was a good idea because no one would want to come here… I should have read more about them. Anyway, I thought if the park closed, we wouldn't have a reason to live here anymore. So we would move back home. I miss my old school and friends. And no offence, but nothing exciting happens in Brookside."

Jessica laughed. "Then you haven't lived here long enough!" Everyone else laughed too.

Chapter Seventeen
Imperfect Ending

Ellie turned her necklace over in her hand as she lay on her coffin bed. It had been a busy day. Vienna the gnome was told she wouldn't be in trouble as long as she shrank Blue back down with de-fertilizer. Lou explained that he had been busy helping Alma prep the park. He'd never meant to make Tink feel ignored. They made plans to work on the invisibility formula in a couple days.

All of the vampires' spots and headaches faded after they were soaked in strawberry water. Jessica called to complain twice already that she smelled absolutely disgusting. Ava also called to thank Ellie, but she said she had to be quick. She was grounded. That made zero sense to Ellie since Ava had helped save the day, but then again, Ava's family made no sense. Ellie couldn't help but feel sorry for Ava. And even Jack. The worst thing Ellie had to deal with in her family was her dad cracking embarrassing jokes, her mother over-worrying, and Penny being pesky.

As if hearing Ellie's thoughts, Penny peeked into the bedroom.

"Ellie, are you busy?" she asked, knocking softly.

"No," said Ellie. "Come in."

Penny skipped in with a bowl of blood pudding in one hand and her favorite teddy, Miss Batty, in the other.

"Does Miss Batty like blood pudding too now?" Ellie asked.

Penny giggled. "Doesn't everyone? But I brought this for you."

"Me? Wait a minute… what did you do to it?"

"Nothing!" Penny insisted. "I thought you might want your favorite snack."

"I'm not hungry, but thanks," Ellie said.

"Woah, are you sick?" Penny asked. "Oh

no, are you trying to be like Tink? I know he thinks blood pudding is gross, but he's wrong!"

Ellie laughed. "No, just not hungry." Her thoughts drifted to her three best friends. She had never been so relieved when she saw they were all okay. This mystery was one of the hardest and scariest. But despite everything, all they could talk about on the way home was their next mystery. She loved her friends.

"Hey, Ellie," Penny said, climbing onto the bed. "About my birthday party." She took a big bite of blood pudding.

Ellie's stomach swelled with guilt. "Look, Penn, I should have never told you I would fix the park. It will be closed for a long time with all the damage, so you won't get to have your birthday there. I'm sorry. Turns out not all mysteries have a perfect ending."

Penny dribbled some pudding on the bed. "Oops," she said, wiping it away. Usually, Ellie would be mad, but not today. "I know," Penny said, surprising Ellie. "Mom explained it to me. She also said we will probably get free tickets for life!"

"Then what did you want to tell me about your birthday?"

Penny shoved more pudding into her mouth. "We're going to have it here, and Mom said I can make it any theme. And I want it to be detective-themed. I was wondering if you could help me make a banner with bats wearing detective hats. Ooo. And maybe help me with a detective costume. I want a turquoise coat, just like yours!"

Ellie's eyes filled with tears. "I can definitely help you with that."

Penny put her bowl down on the end table and crawled into bed with Ellie. She rested her head on her sister's shoulder.

"I think Scaredy Bats make the best big sisters."

Just as Ellie was about to tell her sister she loved her, Penny wiped her sticky pudding moustache on Ellie's arm.

"I also think they make the best napkins!" Penny exclaimed. She jumped up from the bed and ran away.

"I'm going to get you!" Ellie shouted.

“Scaredy Bats also make the best runners.” As she sprang to her feet, her detective notebook spilled open on the floor. Ellie smiled and lowered her voice to a whisper. “And maybe, just maybe, they make the best detectives.”

Are You Afraid of Heights?

Acrophobia [a-kruh-fow-bee-uh] is the intense and persistent fear of heights. It comes from "ákron," the Greek word for peak, summit or edge, and "phóbos," the Greek word for fear.

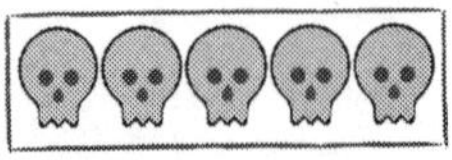

Fear Rating: Acrophobia is one of the most common phobias. People with this phobia can experience feeling dizzy, lightheaded, queasy, shaky, and rapid heartbeats.

Origin: Fear of heights may be caused by an instinctual evolutionary response, a negative or traumatic past experience, and family history.

Fear Facts:

- People with acrophobia may fear walking up stairs, climbing a ladder, crossing a bridge, riding a rollercoaster, and standing at the top of a building.
- The tallest roller coaster is Kingda Ka at Six Flags in Jackson, New Jersey.
- Actor Will Smith faced his fear by going skydiving for his 50th birthday.
- "She was afraid of heights, but she was more afraid of never flying." -Atticus
- Tips: Focus on the horizon or something still, pause, breathe, and distract.

Jokes: What do you call a bird that's afraid of heights?
A chicken.

Fear No More! With preparation and practice, most can manage the fear of heights. But if you believe you suffer from acrophobia and want help, talk to your parents or doctor about treatments. For more fear facts, visit: scaredybat.com/bundle2.

Suspect List

Fill in the suspects as you read, and don't worry if they're different from Ellie's suspects. When you think you've solved the mystery, fill out the "who did it" section on the next page!

Name: Write the name of your suspect

Motive: Write the reason why your suspect might have committed the crime

Access: Write the time and place you think it could have happened

How: Write the way they could have done it

Clues: Write any observations that may support the motive, access, or how

Suspect 1

Draw below

Name:
Motive:
Access:
How:
Clues:

Suspect 2

Draw below

Name:
Motive:
Access:
How:
Clues:

Suspect 3

Draw below

Name:	
Motive:	
Access:	
How:	
Clues:	

Suspect 4

Draw below

Name:
Motive:
Access:
How:
Clues:

Who Did It?

Now that you've identified all of your suspects, it's time to use deductive reasoning to figure out who actually committed the crime! Remember, the suspect must have a strong desire to commit the crime (or cause the accident) and the ability to do so.

For more detective fun, visit:
scaredybat.com/bundle2

Name:
Motive:
Access:
How:
Clues:

Hidden Details Observation Sheet
-- Level One --

1. What lost item were Ellie and Tink trying to find at the start?
2. What got stuck in the tree that Ellie had to retrieve?
3. What new fear did Ellie develop after falling out of the tree?
4. Where did Ellie's sister Penny want to have her birthday?
5. What is happening at the new theme park that could be a mystery?
6. Who was the suspicious hooded person?
7. What normally happens when Jessica sneezes?
8. Where did Ellie and friends find shelter from the rain storm?
9. What type of plant left holes and sap all over the park?
10. What ride did Ellie use to get high enough to reach the plant's mouth?

Hidden Details Observation Sheet
-- Level Two --

1. Where did Ellie find her missing necklace?
2. What was Ellie looking forward to most about Mega Adventureland?
3. What clue did Ellie find that led them to suspect Ava and Jack's mom?
4. What clues revealed the identity of the hooded person?
5. What fruit helped protect the vampires against the headaches and power drain?
6. Who wrote the note that warned the kids to get out of the park?
7. What creature did Ava think she saw in The Smoothie Shack?
8. What happened to the people that got the plant sap on them?
9. What is a gnome's favorite food?
10. What did Ellie throw in the mouth of the Blumungous?

Hidden Details Observation Sheet
-- Level Three --

1. What did Tink use to get the lollipop out of Ellie's hair?
2. What was the name of the plants book in Tink's backpack?
3. What proof did Ava have that her mom wasn't sabotaging the park?
4. What is the name of the competitor theme park?
5. What temporary clue did Ellie see on the sandy floor of The Smoothie Shack?
6. What was in Ava's drawing that was missing in The Smoothie Shack?
7. What flowers inside the park were Typhoon and his snakes allergic to?
8. How long before the people inside the Blumungous stomach would be digested?
9. Who was responsible for growing the Blumungous?
10. What theme did Penny choose for her birthday party?

Answer Key

Level One Answers

1. Ellie's purple dragon necklace
2. Penny's new dragon kite
3. A fear of heights
4. Mega Adventureland
5. Rides are breaking
6. Lou
7. She transforms into a rat
8. The Smoothie Shack
9. Blumungous Flower
10. Roller coaster (Speed Monkey Monster Coaster)

Level Two Answers

1. Attached to Penny's dragon kite
2. Solving the Mega Mystery Mansion
3. Her purple scarf
4. The wrist scar and orange smell
5. Strawberries
6. Lou
7. Green snake
8. They disappeared and transported into the plant's stomach
9. Mustard
10. The bat plushie from Fez

Level Three Answers

1. Fitzgerald's Slick and Sweet Salad Dressing
2. Gnome Sweet Gnome: Cooking with Magic Plants
3. A time-stamped photo strip
4. Typhoon's Terror Park
5. Tiny footprints
6. Purple fruit (plums, grapes)
7. Clovertine flowers
8. One hour
9. Vienna, a young gnome girl (daughter of the park gardener)
10. Detective-themed

Discussion Questions

1. What did you enjoy about this book?
2. What are some of the themes of this story?
3. How did the characters use their strengths to solve the mystery together?
4. What is your favorite theme park ride and why?
5. Can you remember a time when you developed a new fear?
6. How did Ellie overcome her fear of heights?
7. If you could grow a plant that could have any flavor, what would it be?
8. What other books, shows, or movies does this story remind you of?
9. What do you think will happen in the next book in the series?
10. If you could talk to the author, what is one question you would ask her?

For more discussion questions, visit:
scaredybat.com/bundle2

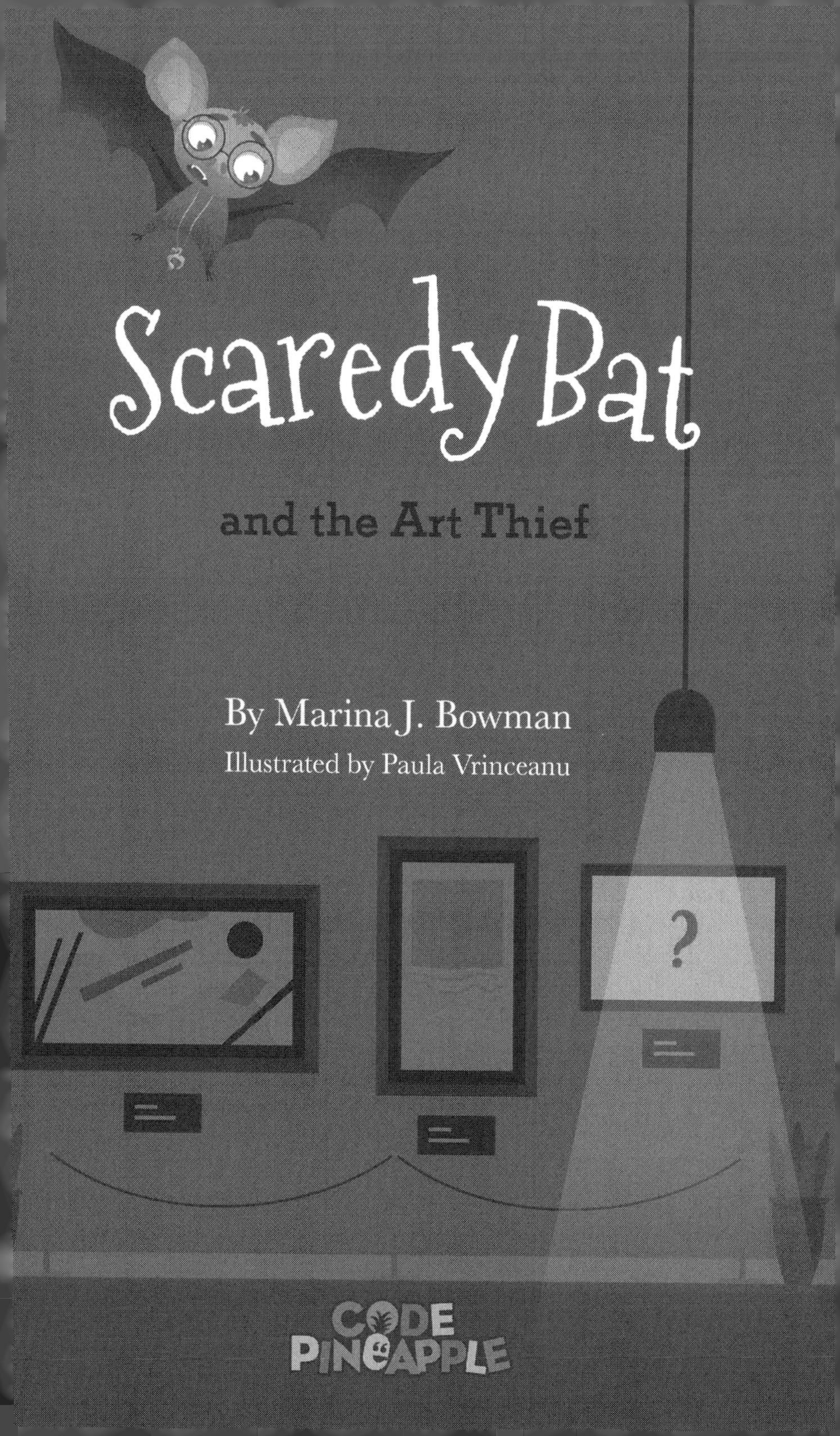
Scaredy Bat
and the Art Thief
By Marina J. Bowman
Illustrated by Paula Vrinceanu
?
CODE PINEAPPLE

Contents

Batty Bonuses

Can you solve the mystery?

All you need is an eye for detail, a sharp memory, and good logical skills. Join Ellie on her mystery-solving adventure by making a suspect list and figuring out who committed the crime! To help with your sleuthing, you'll find a suspect list template and hidden details observation sheets at the back of the book.

There's a place not far from here
With strange things 'round each corner
It's a town where vampires walk the streets
And unlikely friendships bloom

When there's a mystery to solve
Ellie Spark is the vampire to call
Unless she's scared away like a cat
Poof! There goes that Scaredy Bat

Villains and pesky sisters beware
No spider, clown, or loud noise
Will stop Ellie and her team
From solving crime, one fear at a time

Chapter 1
Hide-and-Seek

Creak. Crack. Creak.

The wood stairs groaned as Ellie Spark raced to the attic. With each step, the smell of paint and stale coffee strengthened.

"Eighteen, nineteen, twenty!" came Penny's voice from downstairs. "Ready or not, here I come!"

Sketches and newspaper clippings on a bulletin board flapped and crinkled as Ellie zipped past them. She quickly shoved the whiny rolling chair out from under the long wooden desk. As she tried to squish herself where the seat was, the smell of bubblegum filled her nose. She sniffed the air, tracking the aroma to right above her head. A mosaic of colorful gobs of gum decorated the underside of the desk.

"Ew, Penny," Ellie whispered. Her little sister was always chewing gum when she colored in the attic art studio. Apparently, those chewy morsels were not making it to the garbage. Ellie unstuck one of her long brown strands from a green gob and sought out a less sticky hiding spot.

Creak. Crack. Creak.

Her heart raced at the sound of footsteps on the stairs. She jammed herself behind a red dresser, desperate to not be found by her little sister. After all, this was one game of hide-and-seek she didn't want to lose. The loser owed the winner their portion of dessert all next week. And Ellie was not willing to give up her favorite food ever—ooey gooey blood pudding. She tried to squash herself further behind the dresser, but no matter how hard she squeezed her legs in, her moon socks poked out. She scrambled back to her feet.

Creak. Crack. Creak.

She bolted to the closet, whipping an empty easel with her long turquoise trench coat. It fell to the floor with a *BANG!*

Creak. Crack. Creak.

Out of time, she left the downed easel and dove into the closet jammed with musty old clothes. She tried to quiet her breathing as she peeked through the crack in the door.

Mrs. Spark appeared at the top of the stairs with a fistful of clean paint brushes. Her messy bun bobbed along to whatever tune was blasting through her headphones. She hummed as she stuffed the brushes into the red dresser. Ever since dropping off her painting for the museum's art exhibit, she had been in a great mood.

Ellie let out a sigh of relief. Her eyes trailed the floor-length curtains across the room gently swaying in the breeze. Deciding that would be a much better—and less cramped—hiding spot, she quietly pushed the door open.

Creak. Crack. Creak.

Ellie pulled the closet door shut, once again leaving a small crack to squint through. Penny poked her head into the attic and scanned the studio.

“Mom, have you seen Ellie?” she asked.

Mrs. Spark continued to hum as she organized the drawers.

“Mom?” Penny repeated. “MOM?”

Instead of answering, Mrs. Spark’s humming turned into loud—very offkey—singing. “And with a little bit of red, green, and blue, I’ll find my way back home to you. Oh babyyyyy,” she bellowed into a paintbrush microphone. Her hips swayed side to side. “I’m coming back home to you.”

Ellie covered her mouth to stifle a laugh. In

all of her twelve years, she had rarely seen her mother dance and sing like that. Penny stood at the top of the stairs with her mouth hanging open.

Mrs. Spark belted out another chorus before turning to the stairs with a hip pop, booty shake, and spin.

"Penny!" Mrs. Spark cried, freezing on the spot. Her face flushed red as she took off her headphones. "How long have you been there?"

Penny's white fangs shone as she let out a belly laugh. "Mom, I didn't know you could dance!" Her dress swished as she imitated the booty shake.

Mrs. Spark laughed. "What can I say? I'm full of surprises." She turned back to the dresser. "Did you need something?"

"Have you seen Ellie?" Penny asked.

Mrs. Spark tucked away her makeshift microphone. "No, sorry." She reached down and lifted the easel off the floor. "Whoops, must have knocked this over." She pushed the closet door shut as she walked back to the stairs. As the crack of light disappeared, Ellie and the closet clutter were swallowed by darkness. The door sealed with a *click*.

"Maybe check downstairs," suggested Mrs. Spark.

The two sets of footsteps creaked against the stairs, but Ellie could barely hear them over her heart hammering. Not wanting to lose the game, she waited until they were gone to try to push the door open. But it wouldn't move. She realized that click had been the latch—she was trapped. Her breathing became fast and heavy as panic flooded her body.

"Mom! Mom!" she yelled. "You locked me in!" But there was no answer. The darkness surrounding her was like a snake coiling around Ellie's body. Every second she spent in the pitch-black closet, the tighter the grip felt, and the harder it was to breathe.

Chapter 2

The Unknown Caller

Tears flowed down Ellie's face as she gasped for air in the darkness. She banged on the closet door with her fists.

"Help!" she sobbed. "Get me out of here!" The tightness across her chest made every breath fast, loud, and shallow. She stopped to listen for footsteps over her breathing, but the only sound was the wind whistling through the window across the room.

"HELP!" she yelled once more. "I'm stuck. It's dark, and I can't breathe." Sweat trickled down her forehead as the closet suddenly felt like a scorching hot oven. A few moments later, small creaks and cracks came from the stairs. "I'm in the closet!" Ellie cried. "Open the door!"

"Ha! Found you! I win!" Penny boasted. "I get your blood pudding for a whole week!" The sound of food crunching filled Ellie's ears.

"Yes, you win. Now open the door. It's dark in here, and I can't breathe."

"I think you're just being a Scaredy Bat and pancaking," Penny said. "My friend Libby's mom gets pancake attacks sometimes."

Ellie slammed her fist on the closet door repeatedly. "It's a *panic* attack, not a *pancake* attack. And I don't care what it is. I just want out of here. It's small, dark, and a million degrees. Mom! MOM!" she shouted.

The sound of food crunching once again echoed through the room. "She can't hear you," Penny said with a mouthful. "She has her headphones on."

"Penny. Let. Me. Out!" Ellie said through gritted teeth.

"If I let you out, what do I get?" Penny asked.

"You win and get my blood pudding all next week," Ellie said. "What more do you want?"

"Duh!" Penny exclaimed. "But I want to be let in your room anytime I want for a month."

"Fine! Just open the door." With a click, Penny unlatched the closet. Ellie burst out, taking in loud gasps of stale attic air.

Penny crunched down on the last of her carrot. "Wow, a whole month in your room! You should pancake more often." Ellie lunged toward her sister and chased her around the attic.

"I'm going to make *you* into a pancake," Ellie yelled. They wove around the easel before they scurried down the creaky stairs, all the way to the kitchen.

"Mom! MOM!" Penny cried. "Ellie is chasing me." They slid across the freshly cleaned floors with their sock feet. The smell of lemony cleaner lingered in the air.

Mrs. Spark was holding the phone to her ear. "Shh, I can't hear," she whispered.

"Is it Grandma?" Ellie whispered. "She is supposed to call me back about my necklace." Ellie clutched the purple dragon pendant hanging around her neck.

Mrs. Spark hushed Ellie. "I understand. That is quite the problem," she said to the unknown caller.

Ellie's mind wandered back to her last mystery at the amusement park. A gnome had told her that her necklace was special. Ever since then, she had been trying to learn more about it but couldn't find anything.

"Of course, Ellie is right here," Mrs. Spark said. "If she is interested, she can take her bike there later today." She handed Ellie the phone. "It's for you."

Ellie put it to her ear. "Hello?"

"Hello there, Miss Ellie!" said a chipper male voice. "How are you on this fine day?"

"Good," Ellie answered.

"Excellent," said the caller. "Then I'll cut right to the chase. My name is Henry Beagon from the Brookside Vampire Artifact Museum. And I'm calling because we have a mystery on our hands."

Ellie gasped as her heart fluttered with excitement. "A mystery!?"

"Yes, ma'am, a mystery. And I know that you are the absolute best detective in town, so I had to call you right away. I've already talked to your mother, and she said it would be okay if you and your detective team came down here to help out. That is, of course, if you don't already have plans today."

"No, sir, no plans!" Ellie said, dancing on the spot.

"Perfect! How about we meet at the museum, oh, let's say in an hour, around 3:00? Does that work for your schedule, Detective Ellie?"

"Yes!" Ellie said. "I just need to call my friends to make sure they can come. I will see you at 3:00, Mr. Beagon."

"Looking forward to it." The phone call ended with a click.

"Mom! Someone called ME about a mystery!" Ellie squealed.

Mrs. Spark gave a big, fangy smile. "I heard! Congratulations, Detective Ellie."

"Can I go? Please, please, please!" Penny begged.

"Sorry, Mr. Beagon only asked for me and my detective team." Ellie's face was starting to hurt from smiling so hard. "I have to call Jessica, Fez, and Tink ASAP."

"But I want to go, too!" Penny complained, sticking out her bottom lip.

"You can help me pick an outfit for the art show tonight. It's at the museum, so we can meet Ellie there. I can't wait for you both to see my finished painting on display. Plus, I'll have a special surprise for you girls there." Mrs. Spark's smile faded. "That is, if they don't cancel the exhibit."

"Cancel it! Why would they do that?" Ellie asked.

Mrs. Spark sighed. "Mr. Beagon said they might cancel if they can't solve the mystery. I will have done all that painting for nothing."

Ellie gave her mom a big hug. "It's okay; Detective Ellie is on the case!"

Mrs. Spark squeezed her daughter. "Just remember that you're still my little girl. It's okay if you don't solve *all* the mysteries. There will be plenty that need solving when you're older, but you're only a kid once."

"I know," Ellie said as she dialed the phone. "But I need lots of practice, because I want to be the best detective ever!" Before Mrs. Spark could reply, Ellie was already on her first call. "Hi, Mr. Fitzgerald. Can I talk to Fez, please?"

A few minutes later, Ellie let out a squeal of excitement as she hung up from her last call—all three of her detective friends were free. She dreamed about what the mystery could be as she packed her coat pockets with her notepad, magnifying glass, and fingerprinting kit. Was it some mysterious beast terrorizing the museum? Was there a magical spell that had to be lifted? Ellie hoped it wasn't something like Mr. Beagon misplacing his glasses. Although, she would still be happy to help.

Any mystery was a good mystery. And there was only one way to discover what this one was all about.

Chapter 3

Vampire Artifact Museum

The chilly autumn air was crisp and energizing against Ellie's skin. It was extra refreshing when she peddled her bike up the steep hill to the museum. Halfway up, her legs burned like a million fire ants had stung her all at once. She stopped for a quick break, and to her delight, she was right beside the flyer she'd hung last week. The paper stapled to the wood pole read:

Best Detectives in Brookside. If you have a mystery, we can solve it. Call us today!

Front and center was a silhouette of the detective squad—Ellie, Jessica, Tink, and Fez.

Ellie's purple dragon necklace was still colorful and bright, though. Jessica had said "it will make the poster pop!" However, it was no longer the only color popping—along the bottom was a note scribbled in red marker.

Best detectives? They're just LITTLE KIDS!

Ellie's shoulders slumped. She remembered someone calling her last week about a lost cat. When they'd found out she was a kid, they said their cat "just walked in the door" and hung up. She tore down the flyer, crumpled it, and shoved it in her pocket. She was so tired of people not taking her seriously because of her age.

Not long after she started to peddle again, the museum's tree sculpture peeked over the hill's crest. The cement branches sprawled out from the trunk like spider legs. Each limb was enchanted to bear real fruit. Bright red apples, yellow bananas, and purple lemons called Violems created a rainbow against the gray cement.

Ellie parked her bike beside the gnome sculptures dancing around the tree base. The anger flowing through her melted as her hand wandered to the cool metal on her necklace. One of the dancing gnomes with an apron and moustache looked exactly like the one she'd met at Mega Adventureland.

His words had been replaying in her head ever since: "That's a very special necklace. So rare. I've never seen one in real life." However, he never got a chance to tell Ellie why.

"Concentrate," she whispered to herself. "There will be time to figure out the necklace later." She turned away from the sculpture toward the museum. The red brick of the single-story building was warm and inviting against the dreary autumn sky. The long house with a flat roof and border of hedges was once a Vampire Inn—a secret place that hid traveling vampires from hunters. Once it outlived its purpose, the owner sold it to a museum developer before she left to look for her lost son.

Too excited to wait for the others, Ellie stepped around a massive mud puddle and climbed the stone steps. She ran her hand over

the carvings of the fire-breathing dragons battling water demons on the double doors. The breath of fire intertwined with the blasts of water wrapped around the cool brass door handles. She grabbed the knob and tugged. The door opened without a sound.

A comforting warmth washed over her chilly skin as she stepped inside. The smell of the entrance was lemony fresh, with a hint of flowers—just as she remembered. She couldn't count how many school field trips had been spent here over the years. Although, it got a little boring with very few new artifacts coming into the small museum. Ellie's mother said that was why they'd decided to explore other exhibits, like modern art.

An older man with a black suit and gray slicked-back hair walked toward Ellie. His shoes were almost as shiny as the black marble floors that tapped under his feet.

"You must be Detective Ellie," he said. "So pleased that you could come on such short notice." He gave her a small bow.

Ellie gave him a big, fangy grin. "That's me! And you must be Mr. Beagon."

"Right you are. But please, call me Henry." He tucked his clipboard under his arm and straightened his bowtie. "I was actually one of your grandfather's good friends."

"You were?" Ellie said, her mouth gaping slightly. Ever since her grandfather had passed away a couple years ago, she rarely heard anyone talk about him.

Henry gave a small smile. "I knew Leo for over forty years. I also know your grandmother quite well." He pointed to her necklace. "I recognized your necklace on your detective flyer right away. I remember your grandmother finding it on her Terrascope travels like it was yesterday."

Ellie gasped. "Can you tell me more about the necklace?"

Henry shook his head. "Afraid I don't know much more. I do believe there is some information on it in our Archive Room. But the problem is, I can't find the key. I think whoever took the artwork also stole the key to the archives. They both went missing today."

Ellie pulled her detective notebook from her pocket. "I'm guessing I'm here because of the missing art?" she said.

Henry nodded. "Right you are, Detective Ellie. Now, we should get to work. Follow me to the scene of the crime." Ellie tried to put on a serious face as they stepped into room 1B off to the left. But she couldn't stop smiling. Henry was treating her like a real detective.

An oversized chandelier with glimmering green and blue crystals hung in the middle of the ocean-blue room. She followed Henry as he wove between the round tables draped with orange tablecloths. Each one was set with white plates and blue napkins centered around a vase of velvety black roses. There wasn't a wrinkle or a speck of dust in sight.

Henry arrived at a tarnished silver frame hanging on the wall. It was woven from carvings of branches and snakes. And whatever picture it had once held was ripped out. Pieces of the torn paper inside the frame gently flapped in the breeze from a nearby vent.

"This old painting was going to be the showpiece for the exhibit tonight, but someone tore it out," Henry explained. "We don't want to put any more art in danger, so we are thinking about canceling tonight's event."

Ellie bit her lip. She wanted to tell him he couldn't do that—her mom worked too hard. But she reminded herself that grownup detectives don't let their feelings interfere with a case. Instead, she tried logic.

"But why would the thief come back to steal more art?" Ellie asked "Wouldn't they just take it all the first time?"

"Perhaps," Henry answered. "But our newest exhibit wasn't set up yet. It has a mix of art, including some from very important artists. We just got a shipment with some very valuable pieces today at 2:00."

"When did you notice the art was missing?" Ellie asked as she squinted at the frame.

Henry scratched his stubbly chin. "It disappeared sometime between 11:00 this morning and 2:00 while I was golfing. I noticed it was gone when I got back at 2:05 and called you right away." He groaned. "These events are always so stressful. I wish I didn't have to do them, but fewer and fewer people are visiting the museum since we get so few new artifacts. I really wish vampire families would see the value of putting special pieces on display instead of hoarding them." Ellie nodded and pulled her mom's makeup brush from her coat pocket. "What are you doing?" Henry asked with wide eyes.

Ellie dipped the brush in a small container filled with face powder. "I'm going to dust for fingerprints," she answered. She stepped toward the frame.

"Wait!" Henry cried. "You cannot touch that frame. Even without the art, it is a very valuable artifact." Ellie's face flushed hot with embarrassment.

"Sorry," she mumbled. Ellie tucked the brush in her pocket. She stood up straight as she realized something important. "I don't think someone did this for the art or the art's value," she observed.

"Why do you say that?" Henry asked.

"Because they ripped the painting and left the valuable frame behind," Ellie answered.

Henry grinned. "I knew I picked the right detective for the case. Great observation." He lowered his voice. "I thought of that too, but why else would they do such a thing?"

Ellie pulled out her notebook. "Maybe they wanted to ruin the exhibit tonight."

"Hmm, I think you're on to something," Henry said. He lowered his voice to a whisper. "Our curator, Clara Burg, wanted to submit a piece to the art show. But we have a strict rule about museum employees not participating in exhibits. We just can't risk looking like we have favoritism. Anyway, today is her last day before retiring, so she asked if we could move the exhibit. That way, she could submit a painting. But unfortunately, the date was already

Suspects

1. *Henry Beagon – Hates events. Sabotage?*
2. *Clara Burg – Wanted art exhibit moved*

Clues

1. *Ripped painting*

set. She didn't seem very happy."

Ellie scribbled in her notepad.

"So you think Clara ruined the painting to postpone the event?" Ellie asked.

Henry straightened his bowtie. "It is a possibility. Oh, but sweet Clara. It is so hard to imagine her doing such a thing. She has been with the museum longer than I have. I don't know. What do you think? You're the detective!"

Before Ellie could answer, the sound of laughter interrupted.

"Ellie? Ellie!?" came a loud whisper from the front door. "Sorry we're late."

Chapter 4

Best Detectives in Brookside

Jessica, Fez, and Tink stepped into Room 1B, the dining room.

"There you are!" Jessica said. She took off her hood, shaking out her red curls. "Brr, it sure is chilly out there," she said.

Tink wiped his glasses off on his shirt. "It is actually unseasonably warm today. Although, I still think it is too cold for a slushie." Fez slurped on the swirly straw sticking out of a cup so big that it took two hands to hold.

"No way, it's never too cold for slushies," he said. He licked his lips with his blue tongue. "Especially sour raspberry!"

Henry cleared his throat as his eyes darted

to the mud dripping off the trio's shoes. "I am sorry, the museum is closed today to prepare for the gallery opening tonight," he said. "We would be happy to have you another time. Perhaps when you are a little less muddy." Jessica, Tink, and Fez followed Henry's gaze to the mud trail they'd made.

"Oops, sorry, "Jessica said. "But we're not here for a tour—we're here to solve the mystery."

Henry turned to Ellie. "These are your… associates, Detective Ellie?"

Ellie's mouth felt glued shut as her friends' muddy shoes dripped all over the previously spotless floors. Her face burned as she gave a small nod.

Henry groaned. "Very well, then." He snapped his fingers at Tink, who had pulled a towel from his backpack to mop up the mess. "No need for that." He lifted his boney wrist and spoke into a gold bracelet. "Carter, mud cleanup in Room 1B, ASAP."

"Got it," said a voice from the sparkling jewelry piece.

"Woah, that is awesome!" Tink said. "It's so small and discreet. I didn't know they sold anything that tiny. Do you mind if I see it up close?" he asked.

Henry tucked the bracelet under his sleeve. "Maybe after we—"

Jessica gasped. "Are these Bat Breath Roses?" She ran a thumb over one of the black rose's velvety petals. She put her nose to one. "Wow, they really do smell like sweet cherries."

The loud slurping coming from Fez's straw stopped. "No way! That's so cool." He rushed to take a sniff, putting his drink on the tablecloth.

"No!" Henry squealed, rushing over. "These are super rare and were extremely hard to get for tonight's event." He scooped up the drink, but it was already too late—there was a water ring where the cup had sat.

"Sorry," Fez said with a blue grin, taking back his drink.

Henry whirled around to Ellie. "I am sorry, Miss Spark. Are you sure you and your... friends are up to this task?" He smoothed out the tablecloth. "I am on a ticking clock, and I need the best detectives to solve this case." He looked at Fez, who resumed slurping the slushie. "You advertised yourselves as the best—not sticky little sleuths who are going to touch everything."

"No!" Ellie exclaimed. "We can do this." Jessica stood up a little straighter, smoothing out her purple dress. "What do we know so far?" she asked in a serious voice. Henry repeated what he'd told Ellie and how they didn't think the painting had been stolen for its value or the artwork itself. Tink stepped closer to the painting as he listened. A distant crash and scream pierced the air.

BEEP! BEEP! BEEP!

An alarm blared, and Fez jumped, spilling his slushie on the floor.

POOF! Ellie turned into a bat and flapped up into the chandelier.

Chapter 5

The Easiest Case Yet

Ellie, Jessica, Fez, Tink, and Henry followed the loud alarm to room 3B. They leapt over the mop and bucket in the doorway and into the flashing lights that bathed the art-filled room in an angry red glow. An eighteen-year-old boy with an uneven bowl cut stood in the middle of the chaos. Tucked under his arm was a soccer-ball-sized object. Beside him, an old woman cringed while cupping her ears.

"Henry! Turn this doggone alarm off!" she yelled. "You're going to make me deafer than I already am." Henry ran out of the room, and the wailing alarm and flashing lights stopped within a few seconds. The woman let out a sigh of relief. "Much better." The oversized gems on her rings sparkled as her shaky hands smoothed her dark braids pulled into a bun. Then she picked her tablet off the floor.

"Ah-ha! I think we caught our art thieves!" Fez said. "This was the easiest case yet." The woman and boy exchanged a confused look before bursting into laughter.

"We aren't art thieves—we work here," said the boy. "This is Clara, our art curator. And I'm Henry's grandson, Carter."

"I've worked here since before you youngins were born," Clara added. "If I wanted to steal art, I wouldn't have waited until my last day." She pointed to the ball under Carter's arm. "That head sculpture just came to life as I was hanging the work for tonight's show. One minute it was sittin' on that column all still, then BAM! It jumps off like it was some sort of bouncing bunny."

"Did you see this?" Ellie asked Carter.

"No," Carter answered. "I was grabbing a mop and bucket, but I raced in as soon as I heard the alarm. The alarm is pressure sensitive, so it goes off if anything is removed from the column. That means it would go off if this

guy accidentally got knocked down." Carter held out the sculpted marble head. A deep crack snaked between the eyes and down the nose. A yellow layer of crust sat in the left eye socket.

"*JUMPED* off the column," Clara corrected. "I know I can be clumsy, but this wasn't one of those times. If Henry wasn't so cheap and fixed the camera in this room, I could prove it!" She gave the head a good look, her lips drawing into a hard line. "Oh my, it is completely ruined!" Tears filled her big brown eyes. "This was made by the great Spencer Eve over a thousand years ago. It's priceless." Clara fanned herself. "I think I need to sit down." Carter put the statue back on the podium and put his arm under a wobbly Clara. He led her to a bench under a painting of a duck filming a Ferris wheel filled with parrots.

Fez cringed at the statue's crusty eye socket. "Looks like the poor guy has an eye infection. I had one of those once, and it oozed yellow goop."

"Ew, Fez, TMI," Jessica said, her face turning slightly green. "It just looks like some sort of glue. I've used similar stuff when putting gems on clothing."

"It is glue," Carter confirmed. "This head used to have a big ruby eye before it fell off the column."

Ellie circled the room. Three walls were lined with paintings, and the other had columns with sculpted heads. She weaved between the art pieces—a donkey with a witch hat, a clown wearing a jellyfish as hair, a dragon king with a monocle and mustache.

"Where did the ruby eye go after the statue fell—I mean, jumped?" Ellie asked. "I don't see it anywhere."

"Your guess is as good as mine," Clara said. "As soon as it happened, the alarm went off, and you youngins came racing in." Clara's hands clenched into fists by her side. "Maybe that troublesome ghost stole it! Sam Thomlin is always floating around causing havoc. Ever since that Terrascope exhibit we did a few months ago." She shook her head. "Good for nothin' ghost."

"Good for nothing?" Fez said. "Ghosts are great. They're so cool. Did you know they can disappear and reappear in puffs of smoke?" Clara looked up at Fez with her mouth gaping open.

"Not the time," Tink said behind a fake cough. Fez shrugged.

"Is there a way to find Sam?" Ellie asked.

Carter snickered. "No way. Sam doesn't answer to anyone. He's always just doing his own thing. I envy him. Although, if I were a ghost, I sure wouldn't stick around this boring place."

"Do you think Sam would also rip that painting?" Ellie asked.

Clara gasped as her hand fluttered to her heart. "Is that what happened!? That ghoul ripped the canvas painting in there? Henry wouldn't let me in to see for myself." She scoffed. "He said he didn't want to risk any evidence getting ruined."

Ellie flipped her notepad. "It's not a canvas painting, it's paper. It has bits of paper still flapping in the corners."

Clara pursed her lips. "You're wrong, girlie. I know that it was a canvas painting. I even have a photo here on my tablet." She put on the glasses hanging around her neck and peeked over them at the screen. Then, after a few seconds, she let out a loud grunt. "Carter, how do I work this thing again? I can't keep up with all this new hullabaloo."

Carter pulled up the photos on the tablet. The first was of a man with an eyebrow scar and scruffy beard in front of paintings. The next was him hanging on the chandelier in room 1B.

"Oh no, he didn't!" Clara cried. Photo after photo, it was the same man taking selfies all around the museum. "He did! That pesky ghost filled my whole tablet with self photos! And he deleted the other ones I had." The handful of pictures looped as Clara furiously scrolled.

"Wait! Go back to the one of him beside the marble statue head." Ellie said. She looked at the statue and then at the photo's date—two days ago.

Ellie's mouth fell open. "The broken statue is a fake!"

Chapter 6

Don't Lick the Evidence

Carter, Jessica, Tink, Fez, and Clara stared at Ellie.

"What do you mean the broken statue is a fake?" Fez asked. He squinted at it on the column. "It looks pretty real to me. Wait! Is this some sort of vampire intuition thing?" he asked. Ellie giggled. Fez and Tink were always so curious about vampire life.

"No," Ellie said. "I don't think there is such a thing as 'vampire intuition.' Although, that would be cool! Look at this." She held up the tablet with the selfie of the marble statue and Sam the ghost. "This was taken two days ago. If this is a photo of the real sculpture, this broken one has the ruby eye glued on the wrong side."

Clara clutched her heart. "Oh, this is too much for me." She adjusted one of her sapphire rings as she stood. "I need a cuppa tea to calm down. I'll be in the staff room if you need me."

"This is a great find, Ellie," Jessica said. "But how do we know this one isn't real and the one in the photo is fake?"

Ellie bit her lip. "I don't know. I just know they aren't the same."

"Wait, I know!" Tink said. He tapped the gold plate on the wall. It read:

'Head of Loki' by Spencer Eve

Carved from marble with a genuine ruby eye.

"I get it!" Carter exclaimed. "We can test the marble to see if it's real. I doubt whoever switched the head sprung for real marble. They probably stole the original sculpture for the value. If I could just remember how we learned to test marble at Science Camp..."

"That's it!" Tink exclaimed. "That's where I recognize you from. It was hard to tell with your new haircut! I'm Tink."

"Oh!" Carter said. "I remember you!" He

pushed his heavy, uneven bangs off his forehead. But they instantly popped back into place. He peeked over Tink's shoulder at the door to make sure Clara was gone. "Clara is planning on doing hair after she retires. So I volunteered to be her… test subject. But she's a little shaky with the scissors. Good thing she still gets paid after retirement thanks to the five years of vacation hours she saved."

"Not to interrupt, but can we get back to the investigation?" Ellie asked, tapping her foot impatiently. "How can we test the marble?"

"I must have something in here," Tink said. He plopped his backpack on the floor. Both boys knelt down and dug inside excitedly, like dogs looking for their favorite toy.

"Woah, it's like there are two Tinks," Fez whispered.

"I know," Jessica said. "Super freaky."

Ellie smirked. "Hopefully this means whatever they're about to do will go twice as fast."

"Ah-ha!" Tink exclaimed. He held up a small bottle of vinegar. "This will do the trick." He put a few drops on the statue head

and watched closely. "If it is real marble, it will bubble." They observed the drops for over a minute, but they were still.

"No bubbles," Tink concluded. "I don't think it's real."

Carter pulled a fork from the backpack. "Just to double-check your hypothesis, let's try to scratch it." He ran the prong across the sculpture's forehead. "Exactly as I thought, it doesn't scratch easily."

"That means it isn't real marble. Right?"

Fez asked.

"Bingo," said Carter.

"Does that mean that ruby on the floor over there is fake too?" Fez asked. He pointed to a red stone jammed in the heating grate.

"You found it!" Ellie cheered. She plucked up the hot, sticky gem and held it to the light.

"Every side is super scratched. That means it's real. Right?" Ellie said.

Carter shook his head. "Nope. Rubies are the opposite of marble—real ones don't scratch easily." Fez began loudly smelling the air. He sniffed all the way to Ellie's hand, grabbed the gem, and gave it a lick.

"Fez, don't lick the evidence!" Jessica exclaimed.

"I knew I smelled strawberry!" Fez said. "This is just candy."

"I guess that is one very unique way of figuring out what it is," Carter said. Everyone laughed.

"This is a great clue!" Ellie exclaimed.

"And a delicious one," Fez said, giving the fake eye one last sniff before handing it to Ellie.

Ellie held the sticky treat in her hand. "Now we just have to figure out what this has in common with the stolen painting. Let's get to work!"

Chapter 7

Emergency!

After looking over the ghost selfie and the fake statue head once more, Ellie jotted down her new clues and suspects.

Suspects

1. *Henry Beagon – Hates events. Sabotage?*
2. *Clara Burg – Wanted art exhibit moved*
3. *Sam Thomlin's ghost – Stole real head to cause mischief?*

Clues

1. *Ripped painting*
2. *Fake marble head*

Jessica peeked over Ellie's shoulder. "Why would someone ruin one piece of art and switch the other?" she asked.

"That's what I'm trying to figure out," Ellie answered. "Unless... Do you remember how Clara insisted that the other painting was canvas?" Jessica nodded. "Maybe that ripped painting wasn't real. What if someone is stealing the artifacts and breaking fake ones, so no one goes looking for the originals?"

Jessica stared at her best friend. "Ellie, that's genius! You're getting really good at this detective stuff."

"Or maybe they didn't plan on the statue breaking," Tink said. "After all, if the statue didn't break, maybe no one would have figured out it was fake."

"We would have figured it out in our weekly scan," Carter said. He looked up at the detective team, who were giving him blank stares. "Whoops, you're not supposed to know about that," he whispered.

"Why? What's a weekly scan?" Jessica asked.

Carter shushed her. "Keep your voice down. I'll tell you, but you didn't hear it from me. All artifacts that came into the museum when it first opened were embedded with a rice-sized chip. These chips inhibit any magic from accidentally activating but are also supposed to allow us to track them if they're ever stolen."

Tink's mouth fell open. "You altered ancient artifacts!? But can't that ruin them?"

"Keep your voice down," Carter whispered. "That's how many people felt, so the program got scrapped and no tracking was ever added. It wasn't worth trying to remove the chips from objects that already had them, and certain metal scanning wands can detect them. My grandfather is overly paranoid and insists we scan all items with a chip weekly to make sure they're the real deal."

"Can't someone just put a chip in a fake item?" Tink asked.

"No," Carter answered. "The chips were made of a rare metal that is nearly impossible to find now."

"Does that ripped painting have a chip?"

Ellie asked.

"Nope," Carter answered.

"Then we need to test it another way. C'mon, guys!" Ellie said to the group of boys. "We might need more of your science-y stuff."

Carter started to follow but quickly paused. "I would love to—this is the most exciting thing to ever happen in this boring place. But I need to stay here and clean up this mess. My grandfather will be mad if I don't." He gave a weak smile. "Good luck." Tink scanned the pieces of broken statue on the ground.

"Is it alright if I stay and help?" he asked Ellie. "I just want to catch up quickly, then I'll be back on the case."

Ellie groaned. "Tink, we're supposed to be investigating. This isn't very professional."

"It will only be a few minutes," Tink said. "I'm sure I won't miss much." Before Ellie could respond, Tink was already bent down, picking up chunks of stone. Annoyance zipped through her like a lightning bolt. And a faint squeaking off in the distance wasn't helping her irritation.

Fez put a hand on Ellie's back. "It's okay. We can start without him. Let's go."

The trio ran down the hall. Loud voices boomed from behind a door marked 'Staff Only.' Jessica and Fez kept going, but Ellie paused.

"I know you've never picked up a paint-brush in your life. But these artists worked real hard on their pieces," Clara shouted inside. "If someone is hurting the art, you need to cancel the event. That missing statue head is a price-less vampire artifact, Henry. Priceless! Maybe

you don't appreciate that because you're a human, but it is a piece of our history. It's from a time when vampires were so busy running that they barely had time to make art. It was a symbol of hope for the future of my kind. It's a huge loss to the Brookside community."

"I'm just as devastated as you," Henry said. "I think you forget I've worked my whole life collecting vampire artifacts. I am not taking this lightly. But it is too late to cancel. Let's give the vampire girl a chance."

Clara sighed. "She's a mighty smart kid, but Charles, she's just that. She's just a kid."

Ellie's stomach sank, and tears filled her eyes.

"For the millionth time, I don't like to be called Charles," Henry huffed.

"And I don't like to be disturbed during tea. So shoo," Clara said. "But think about what I said. *Henry*." With the sound of footsteps approaching the door, Ellie dove behind a nearby suit of armor. The words "she's just a kid" echoed in her head as Henry stomped past. With each repetition, her heart ripped apart further. She wiped the tears dripping down her face and whipped open her notebook. Beside Clara's name she wrote *#1 Suspect!*

Jessica ran out of room 1B, her shoes screeching on the polished tile.

"Ellie! Emergency! Emergency!" she shouted. "The frame is gone!"

Chapter 8

Déjà Vu

Ellie rushed into room 1B with Jessica. Fez was staring at the blank wall where the ripped painting had hung before. He pulled a powdered donut hole out of his pocket and stuffed it in his mouth.

"Fez, you aren't supposed to be eating in here," Ellie hissed. "Real detectives don't snack on the case." Fez wiped his powder-covered fingers on his pants.

"Real detectives aren't doing it right then," he said with stuffed cheeks.

Squeak. Squeak. Squeak.

"You know detective work makes me snacky," he continued.

Ellie raised her finger to her lips. "Shh. Listen."

Squeak. Squeak. Squeak.

She tracked the faint sound to the wall. Just as soon as the trio pushed their ears against it, a distant crash boomed in the distance.

BEEP! BEEP! BEEP! The alarm went off.

"Woah, déjà vu!" Jessica yelled over the siren. Before they could leave the room to investigate, Tink raced in.

"The statue broke because it has a flip plate wired underneath!" he yelled. "Carter and I saw it. The top of the podium tipped, the statue head went flying, and the alarm started." The alarm turned off, and Tink took a deep breath. "Wait, where did that painting go?" he asked. They explained the missing painting and the squeaking sound.

Henry barged into the room. "What is happening?" he demanded. He gasped at the sight of Fez eating donuts. He pinched the bridge of his nose and squeezed his eyes shut. "I know that I did NOT just see you eating a powdered donut hole in my event room."

Fez froze, then shook his head. He went to shove the donut back in his pocket but dropped

it on the floor. A puff of white dust revealed a red laser in front of where the painting used to hang. Henry opened his eyes just as the dust settled.

"Noooo," he squealed, looking at the powdery mess. "This room was pristine. Perfect. A work of art before you came in. Wait, where is the painting frame!?"

Ellie gulped. "We just noticed it was missing."

Henry puffed out his cheeks and exhaled

sharply. "I can't, I just can't. We will close the art room for tonight's event. People will enjoy the food and music." He plucked a black flower, put it to his nose, and inhaled deeply. "And these beauties."

Clara stood at the door. "Hallelujah! Now you're thinking," she said.

"But we just found a new clue!" Ellie exclaimed. "And some of those artists have been looking forward to having their art displayed!" Her heart ached thinking how sad her mother would be.

"I. Don't. Care!" Henry screamed. "Nothing is worth this—this mess." He lifted his small gold bracelet to his mouth. "Carter, print out new schedules for tonight. Remove the art room opening."

Carter groaned. "You sure you don't want to just close the museum until we figure this out? Maybe today can also be my last day in this boring place."

"We are not discussing this now," Henry said. "Get moving."

"Hold on," Jessica said. "Don't get rid of

the old schedules. If we solve this case, *which we will*, then you can open the exhibit."

Henry pinched the bridge of his nose. "Fine."

"I like this girl!" Clara clucked from the doorway. "She's fiery, just like her red locks. This is the first time I've seen Henry agree to someone else's idea in a long time. He's an old stubborn mule!" She took a shaky sip of tea.

"But I heard you say you also want to cancel!" Ellie blurted out. "Which would make sense, since you can participate if they move the show."

Clara waved her hand dismissively. "I wanted to cancel before we had a way to protect the art. I think this is a great plan. And even if we reschedule, the art is already picked, so this wouldn't be my show." She gave her bottom a shake. "At this point, I'm just ready to get my party on after my last day of work."

Ellie couldn't help but smirk at the woman's sunny attitude. She pulled out her notepad and scratched Clara's name off her suspect list. If she still couldn't take part in a postponed art show, she had no motive to get it canceled. However, the case did have a new suspect.

Suspects

1. *Henry Beagon – Hates events. Sabotage?*
2. ~~*Clara Burg– Wanted art exhibit moved #1 SUSPECT!*~~
3. *Sam Thomlin's ghost – Stole real head to cause mischief?*
4. *Carter Beagon – Wants museum shut down because it's boring*

Clues

1. *Ripped painting (Missing)*
2. *Fake marble head (on remote controlled flip plate)*

"I have an event security team and caterers to let in," Henry said as he made his way to the door. "You have until 5:00 to figure this out. And please, no more messes." The clock on the wall read 4:00, giving them an hour.

Clara left too, but not before asking Fez for a powdered donut hole. He happily gave her one. As she dusted her hands, the red laser once again appeared.

"I think that may be a tripwire," Tink said once they were alone again. "You guys said you were by the wall when the alarm went off the second time. I was standing by the wall the first time. And if the laser is connected to the statue flip plate, that explains it."

"But what is the point?" Ellie asked.

"Maybe to lure us out of the room," Fez said. "So they could steal the frame."

"Why not just steal the frame when they ripped the painting?" Jessica asked.

"Maybe it was too heavy, so they needed more time? It is made of metal," Ellie answered.

"I hate to say this," Tink said. "But I am starting to suspect Carter. He is really good with technology and could have easily done this. Plus, he is always complaining about how boring it is here."

Ellie nodded. "Me too." Jessica lifted her shoe off the ground.

"Ick, what is so sticky on this floor!" she asked. She slipped off her shoe to look at the bottom. The white rubber had a layer of blue. The zingy smell of sour raspberry filled Ellie's nose.

"Oops," Fez said. "I think that is my slushie from earlier. The first alarm made me spill it." As the sun peeked out from a cloud through the window, it illuminated the floor. Sticky shoe prints smudged the tile. They trailed from where the painting had once hung to the room's door.

"I bet you those belong to the art thief!" Ellie said. She looked at the zig-zag pattern on Jessica's shoe sole. "These flat prints don't match Jessica's shoes. And no one else that we know of walked to the front of the room and back out." She followed the steps out into the hall, where they disappeared into the dark floor. Even with the shiny polish, the pattern made the steps impossible to follow.

"Looks like a dead end," Tink groaned.

"Hold on," Jessica said. "I have an idea. Fez, do you have any more pocket donuts?"

Chapter 9

Do Not Enter

Jessica sprinkled the donut's powdered sugar onto the black tile.

"What are you doing?" Ellie cried. "We aren't supposed to be making more messes."

Fez scowled. "Or wasting donut powder!"

"Hold on," Jessica said. She bent down and blew at the powder. The once-hidden footprint showed up like magic. "The powder sticks to the shoe prints," Jessica explained.

"That's genius!" Tink said. "You know, you could make a good scientist."

Jessica laughed. "Nah, that's your thing. Plus, I actually learned to do this by gluing glitter to clothes—ah-ah-achoo!" Jessica sneezed, and *POOF*, she turned into a rat.

Fez squealed with delight. "Sanalamia.

I will never ever, ever get sick of you transforming into a cute rat. I love that your vampire powers make it happen every time you sneeze." He popped her into the pocket with powdered sugar. "Whoops!" He pulled her back out and blew off her little paws. "Sorry," he whispered before putting her into the other pocket.

Fez took over the powder sprinkling, and they followed the prints all the way down the hall. Across from an office with a nameplate that read "Charles Henry Beagon" was a half-open metal door. In the middle hung a sign that said "Do Not Enter."

Ellie looked at her friends and gulped as they quietly slipped inside. The door closed with a soft click behind them.

Stepping over chunks of missing wood floor, they walked past a grand piano centered under a domed ceiling sparkling with stars. The surrounding walls were clad with dark wood bottom panels. On top were faded, painted murals. The footprints disappeared into a wall with vampires on one side under a starry night sky. On the other were humans in front of a fiery sun. Lemon trees and bags of flour were scattered throughout the human side. On the vampire side were juicy red apples and plump grapes.

"Maybe the ghost walked through the mural," Tink said. "But then again, the frame can't just disappear through the wall."

"Woah, what is this mural?" Fez asked. He ran his finger over the gold line that divided the two species.

"It shows the war between vampires and humans," Ellie explained. "Before we started to live in harmony. This museum actually used to be a Vampire Inn, a place where vampires could hide from humans hunting them. On our last school field trip, they told us this room is where they used to throw parties to try to cheer up the families on the run. When the door of this room and the event room are shut, they are completely soundproof. There used to be live music and dancing almost every night."

Tink shook his head. "It's crazy to think some people still believe we should live separately. If that were true, we would never all be friends."

Fez's shoulders slumped. "But you guys are my best friends. I don't know what I would do without you. There would be no mystery solving. And I wouldn't get to see my vampire friends transform into cute bats and rats." He took Jessica out of his pocket and hugged her against his face. She nibbled his nose.

"Aw, it's a love bite," Fez said. Jessica jumped out of his hands and scurried along the floor.

Tink giggled. "I think it might be more of a 'put me down' bite."

Ellie's eye wandered to a woman hugging a man in the middle of the painting. She couldn't see her face, but in her hand dangled a necklace.

"That's my purple dragon necklace!" Ellie cried. Tink squinted at the art and then at Ellie.

"You sure? That could be any purple pendant. It's kind of blurry."

"It's sort of small, but it looks just like mine!" Ellie said.

“Umm, guys,” Fez said. They looked over just in time to see Jessica squeeze her furry butt into a small crack in the wall.

“Jess, get back here!” Ellie said. “You don’t know what is in there. There could be spiders, or termites, or—”

CRASH! A loud bang thundered in the wall.

“Jess? Jessica!” Ellie cried. “Are you okay?” The only sound in the room was the three friends’ heavy breathing.

“Jessica?” Fez cried. He tugged at the wood panel, but it wouldn’t budge. Tink pulled at a metal candlestick on the wall.

“If we can get this off, we can use it to rip open the hole to get to her!” he said.

“Achoo! I’m okay,” came a quiet voice inside the wall. “The hole collapsed, so I can’t get back out, though. And woah!” Jessica paused. “You aren’t going to believe what is in here. Ah-ah-achoo!” She sneezed and turned back into a rat.

After fifteen minutes, Jessica was still trapped. They tried pushing on panels and searching for a button, key, or anything to get inside. They found a keyhole hidden in the mural, but no key anywhere.

"We need to see if there is some other way to open the door," Tink said. "Maybe a backup in case the key is lost. Or, in our case, can't be found." Fez's stomach grumbled, and Tink shot him a look.

"Sorry, staring at all the apples and fruit on this mural is making me hungry."

"Wait, what do you think this carving in this tree means?" Ellie asked. "'Sing to the stars for the key. Start with apple, apple, grape, grape. Then two times something lemony.'"

"Achoo!" came a sneeze from the other side of the wall. Jessica sighed. "I'm never getting out of here, am I?"

Fez stood up straight. "I'll get you out." He tipped his head to the ceiling and started singing. "Apple, apple, grape, grape, something lemony, lemony. This is my song for the starrr-rrs." With no better idea, all the friends joined in. After a few choruses of nothing happening, they looked for a new plan.

"Hold on, there are apples in this painting,"

Ellie said. She located a bunch and took out her magnifying glass. "And there is some sort of music note written on this one."

Fez peered through the glass. "That's a G note." Next, they located a lemon with an E note and grapes with a D note. Ellie and Tink looked at each other and shrugged.

"I'm not very good at music," Tink said.

"Me neither," Ellie said. "I have no idea what this means." Fez pulled the bench out from the piano in the middle of the room and took a seat.

"I think I know!" he said. He hit the keys one by one—G, G, D, D, E, E. The tune to "Twinkle Twinkle Little Star" floated through the room. The stars on the ceiling grew brighter with each note.

Squeak. Squeak. Squeak.

The wall panel lifted with the final note, revealing the secret room with a soft blue glow.

Jessica ran out. "I had no idea you could play music!" she said. "That was so good."

"Thanks," Fez said with a smile. "The pigs on the farm used to like it when I played for them."

She laughed. "That story doesn't surprise me one bit. Now come on."

Chapter 10

Intruder Alert

Ellie, Jessica, Tink, and Fez crammed into the secret room. One of the security monitors mounted to the wall read 4:30, which meant they only had thirty minutes left to solve the mystery. The screens' light bathed the desk scattered with electronic parts in a blue glow. And in the corner were the frame and marble statue head.

"We did it!" Ellie said. "Whoever has access to this secret room is probably our thief." Tink picked up a screwdriver off the desk.

"I think we know who it is," he said.

"And who it isn't," Jessica said. "Look at this letter. It's from the Museum Board and says that if Henry doesn't bring in money from events this year, they will replace him."

Ellie pulled out her notepad. "If that's true, there is no way he would want to sabotage the event. He seems to care about this place a lot. He freaks out every time something gets a little dirty."

Suspects

1. ~~*Henry Beagon – Hates events. Sabotage?*~~
2. ~~*Clara Burg– Wanted art exhibit moved #1 SUSPECT!*~~
3. *Sam Thomlin's ghost – Stole real head to cause mischief?*
4. *Carter Beagon – Wants museum shut down because it's boring*

Clues

1. *Ripped painting (Missing)*
2. *Fake marble head (on remote controlled flip plate)*
3. *Secret room with monitors and stolen artifacts*

Fez peeled back the ripped paper in the frame. Underneath was a colorful field with a couple sitting on the edge.

"The real painting was underneath the whole time," he said. On one monitor, Carter mopped the sticky footprints off the floors. On another, Henry was locking up the archive room.

"Wait, can you rewind these security cameras to get proof?" Ellie asked. "This isn't looking good for Carter, but good detectives always need evidence." After looking around

the monitors, Tink shook his head. "These aren't the kind that record. They only have a live feed."

Squeak. Squeak. Squeak.

The gang whirled around to find the door closing. It fell closed with a thump just as the security monitors turned off. They were enveloped with darkness.

"What just happened?" Jessica asked.

"Hold on, I have a flashlight," Tink said. The sound of her friends' voices soothed Ellie. Being in the dark with them was always much easier than being alone. Although, she was edgier than usual. The hairs on the back of her neck stood up as her necklace slid upward.

"Got it!" Tink said, flicking on a flashlight. Ellie, Tink, Fez, and Jessica screamed. A man with a scar running across his eyebrow stood beside Ellie. He snagged the necklace and disappeared in a puff of smoke.

Jessica's breath heaved. "Did you see that?"

"Yes," Tink said. "We have to get out of here."

"But my necklace!" Ellie yelled. "The ghost

stole it!"

"Shh!" Jessica said. "You're being loud."

"It's a soundproof room—it's not like Carter can hear us," Ellie huffed.

"Either way, Tink is right," Jessica said. "Look for something to open that door." They ripped through the parts on the desk and crawled underneath but didn't find anything. After a minute of digging around, Fez spoke.

"Found it!" He pushed a red button by the door.

"Intruder alert, intruder alert," blared a voice over the speakers. A whiny alarm screeched through the room.

"I am so sick of alarms!" Jessica said, covering her ears.

"If Carter didn't know we were here before, he does now," Tink said.

Chapter 11

Millions of Messes

The four friends scurried around the cramped room, searching for something to open the door.

"Okay, plan B," Jessica said. She pointed to a vent on the wall. "We crawl out."

"What is that pesky alarm?!" bellowed Clara. It sounded like she was right outside the secret door. They quickly unscrewed the grate and climbed in. The metal shaft squeaked and groaned with each movement.

"This isn't our quietest escape," Jessica whispered. They made it around a corner before the vent cracked underneath them. They tried to crawl faster, but the end of the open shaft crashed through the ceiling. They slid down and fell onto bags full of flour. They coughed and spluttered as puffs of the white powder blocked their view.

"Achoo!" Jessica sneezed and turned into a rat just as Henry appeared through the cloud of dust. His face was redder than the tomatoes on the metal table beside him. The caterers putting together trays stood with their mouths gaping.

"Get. Out!" Henry yelled. "You and your sticky drinks, powdered donuts, and millions of other messes are never to come to this museum again. You're fired!"

"But you don't understand," Ellie said. "Someone stole my necklace, and we think Carter—"

Henry shoved the group to the front door. "I don't care to hear your stories. I should have never trusted a silly little kid."

"Hey, that's not fair!" Fez shouted. "Ellie is—"

"Kicked out forever, as are the rest of you. Now goodbye," Henry snarled. He slammed the doors behind the trio on the front steps. Tears stung Ellie's eyes as she ran to the tree sculpture.

"Ellie, it's okay," Fez said.

"It is not!" Ellie cried. "I was finally getting taken seriously, and you guys had to ruin it. Fez and your drinks and food everywhere. And Tink, you were so busy with Carter that you were missing important parts of the mystery. It was so unprofessional."

"Woah, if I hadn't stayed back to help him, we may have never figured out the statue flipping thing," Tink said. "And Fez's snacks revealed important clues."

Ellie ignored him and scribbled in her detective notes.

Suspects

1. ~~Henry Beagon – Hates events. Sabotage?~~
2. ~~Clara Burg– Wanted art exhibit moved #1 SUSPECT!~~
3. *Sam Thomlin's ghost – Stole real head to cause mischief? Stole my necklace!!!*
4. *Carter Beagon – Wants museum shut down because it's boring*

Clues

1. *Ripped painting (Missing)*
2. *Fake marble head (on remote controlled flip plate)*
3. *Secret room with monitors and stolen artifacts*

Fez patted Ellie's head. "You should be happy. We figured out that Carter was behind it. We solved the mystery."

Ellie moved away from the gesture. "No. Something feels off," she said. "Carter does all this so he doesn't have to work at the museum? How does that relate to the ghost that stole my necklace?"

"Maybe they're unrelated," Tink suggested. Fez snapped a picture of the museum with a black and silver camera.

Ellie shook her head. "My detective gut is telling me they're connected somehow."

Fez circled the tree. "Guys, we lost Jessica. I think she turned into a rat and is still inside!"

"Now we lost Jessica. Great!" Ellie said sarcastically. "What if she can't get out? Or what if one of us squished her falling out of the vent!" She ran back to the front door and gave it a tug, but it was locked. Next, she raced to the side of the brick building and tried to see through the windows. One by one, she scanned the rooms, but there was no Jessica. She squinted into an office with pasty green wallpaper, a portrait of a squirrel wearing a crown, and two desks. Suddenly, a rat scurried over her foot.

"Jessica!" Ellie squealed. She scooped up the furry creature and hugged it. "I thought I lost you."

"Gee, must be nice not to be yelled at," Tink mumbled.

Fez kicked a cluster of crunchy leaves. "Right?" Ellie's stomach sank as she thought back to what she had said to them a couple minutes ago.

"I'm sorry I was mean," she said. "I hate that people just think I'm a little kid so I can't be a real detective. It was nice to be treated like a grownup for once. But here I am, acting like a kid blaming you guys."

Tink sighed. "I get it. Most people don't take me seriously when I'm doing science experiments either."

Fez scratched rat Jessica under the chin. "But guys, don't we have our whole lives to be taken seriously? I kind of just want to have fun and be a kid!"

Ellie smirked. "That's true. I'll try to remember that next time I'm frustrated." A tap came from the inside of the office window, causing the three friends to jump. Jessica opened the window.

"Hurry up. I could only turn the window alarm off for a minute or two." Ellie wrinkled her nose as she held up the rat she was petting. She placed it in the grass, and it scurried away.

"Wait, we can still be friends!" Fez called after it.

"Shh!" Jessica said. "Get in so we can search for evidence to prove it was Carter. You can make friends with random rats later."

When they were all inside, Ellie threw her arms around Jessica. "I'm so happy you're okay."

"Of course I'm okay," Jessica said. "And I can't believe you thought I was that rat. I'm way cuter." They all laughed.

"Now let's find some evidence!" Tink said.

Chapter 12

C.B.

The four friends started their office search in the bigger desk's drawers. Pencils and pens were lined up in neat rows, and papers were perfectly stacked. The smaller desk was the opposite, with piles of messy papers, gum wrappers, and a moldy box of biscuits.

Ellie turned to the seashell clock on the wall. There were only fifteen minutes before people arrived at the art show. And she bet they wouldn't be allowed in the art room. The image of her sad mother floating through her head made her heart ache. She tugged at a filing cabinet, but it was locked. Next, she pulled out her detective notebook and scanned it for inspiration.

Suspects

1. ~~*Henry Beagon – Hates events. Sabotage?*~~
2. ~~*Clara Burg– Wanted art exhibit moved #1 SUSPECT!*~~
3. *Sam Thomlin's ghost – Stole real head to cause mischief? Stole my necklace!!!*
4. *Carter Beagon – Wants museum shut down because it's boring*

Clues

1. *Ripped painting (Missing)*
2. *Fake marble head (on remote controlled flip plate)*
3. *Secret room with monitors and stolen artifacts*

They flipped through books on the shelf looking for secret papers slipped inside or hidden passageways. When that didn't work, they searched through the trash. They dug through tissues, wrappers, and other odd and ends but didn't find anything useful.

As Fez bent down to tie his shoe, a donut slipped out of his pocket and rolled under the big desk. "Whoops," he whispered. He picked it up, gave it a blow, and popped it in his mouth. Jessica cringed and stuck out her tongue. "What? Five-second rule," he said.

Jessica giggled. "At least wipe the evidence away." She got down on her hands and knees and brushed the powder off the carpet. Just then, a shiny metal key taped to the bottom

of the desk caught her eye. "I think I found the filing cabinet key!" she exclaimed. With a click, the drawer rolled open.

"We need to find something that proves Carter did this. Or that he partnered with Sam Thomlin," Ellie said. "Look for something with Sam's name or Terrascope Travels."

Jessica thumbed through the files and paused halfway through.

"What about one with your name?" she asked Ellie. She pulled out a file labelled "E. Spark" and took out the contract inside. It was signed by the initials S.T and C.B. They read it over silently, and Fez clicked a picture with a camera.

Jessica blinked rapidly from the blinding flash. "Where did you get a camera?" she asked.

"It was in that secret room," Fez mumbled. "I accidentally took it. But it's so cool! It must be super old. Is it so wrong to steal from someone that steals?"

"Yes!" Ellie, Jessica, and Tink said in unison.

Fez groaned. "But what if it has some

evidence on it? Then can I keep it?"

Jessica grabbed the camera and turned it over in her hand. "It's an old camera with film, so it would have to be developed. We don't exactly have time or tools to do that right now. It's a good idea, but you still have to give it back."

Fez slumped as he grabbed the camera. "Fine."

Tink flipped to the next page of the contract. "Woah, this is proof," he said. "C.B. signed this contract with S.T. C.B must be Carter Beagon, and S.T is Sam Thomlin. It states that Carter will give Sam certain artifacts if Sam gets him… Ellie's necklace."

Ellie grasped her bare neck. "What!? Why would Carter want my necklace?"

The office door burst open. Carter stepped inside with his arms crossed. "You tell me."

Chapter 13

Proof

Carter shut the door behind him, and the mystery team backed away.

"I know my grandfather kicked you all out, so how did you get back in here?" No one answered. Carter ran his hands through his uneven mushroom cut. "Fine, then tell me what you think I did. You think I stole some necklace? I could hear you through the door." Ellie stepped forward onto the cushy area rug. Her hands shook as she planted them on her hips.

"That's exactly what we think," she said. The contract shook like a leaf in her hands as she picked it up. "And we—we have the proof. These are your initials."

Carter snatched the contract. "I didn't sign this. Someone else with the same initials must have." Everyone was quiet as he read over the contract. Until soft chewing came from Fez popping donut holes in his mouth.

"How deep are your pockets?" Tink asked.

"Deep!" Fez said with a mouthful.

"You know those touched my little rat feet when you put me in your pocket, right?" Jessica asked.

Fez popped another in his mouth and shrugged. "Doesn't bother me."

Carter shushed them. "Wow, whoever did sign this contract is in a lot of trouble," he said.

"Why should we believe it wasn't you?" Jessica asked.

Carter scratched his head. "For one, I want nothing to do with necklaces or other old trinkets. I want to work on new stuff. The only reason I'm still here is because I love spending time with my grandpa. I don't know how to break it to him that I don't want to work in the museum. Truth is, I am taking an electronics internship this January." He placed the contract back on the desk. "You know, you think he would understand. He loves technology just as much as I do. He's the one who taught me everything I know. He should be proud."

"So that secret room with the video monitors isn't yours?" Ellie asked.

"The what?" Carter laughed. "I can't even get my own office around here, let alone a secret room."

"I thought this was your office," Jessica said.

Carter shook his head. "Nope, Clara shares it with my grandfather."

After Carter showed Ellie a document of how he wrote his initials, she scratched his name off her suspect list. While his 'C' had a crooked swoop, the one on the contract was so symmetrical it looked like a computer could

Clues

1. *Ripped painting (Missing)*
2. *Fake marble head (on remote controlled flip plate)*
3. *Secret room with monitors and stolen artifacts*

Suspects

1. ~~Henry Beagon – Hates events. Sabotage?~~
2. ~~Clara Burg– Wanted art exhibit moved #1 SUSPECT!~~
3. Sam Thomlin – Stole real head to cause mischief? Stole my necklace!!!
4. ~~Carter Beagon – Wants museum shut down because it's boring~~

have typed it.

Ellie looked back at the name 'Clara Burg.' "Wait, Clara has the initials C.B."

"And she really likes jewelry," Jessica added. "She could have even stolen the statue head for the ruby."

"I think your best bet is going to talk to her," Carter said. "If she does have your necklace, she is heading out of town tomorrow. You need to catch her before it's too late."

"But aren't you going to tell on us for sneaking back inside?" Ellie asked.

"Yeah right," Carter said. "This is the most interesting day at the museum ever. I want to see how this turns out. Follow me. I know where she is." Ellie stood still, unsure.

"Trust him," Tink whispered. With a deep breath, Ellie did just that. They followed Carter down the hall, and Ellie tried not to stare at how uneven his bowl cut was in the back. She couldn't imagine cutting hair would go well for Clara with such shaky hands. Her mind shot back to the contract's straight and clean initials, and her heart skipped a beat.

"I think we might be wrong about Clara—" she started. But the sight of Henry crossing the hall made them all scramble. Ellie stumbled into knight armor. Then, with a *thunk* and a crash of metal, her elbow smashed into a brick. The wall opened, swallowing her and the knight. She screamed as she slid down the slope into the damp, chilly basement. Then, just as quickly as the secret wall chute had opened, it closed.

Ellie was enveloped in darkness.

Chapter 14

Knight in Shining Armor

Ellie stood, shaking and alone in the pitch-black basement.

"Hello? Hello!" she yelled, but no one seemed to hear her. "Henry is behind this!" she called out. "You need to stop him before he gets away with the necklace. His real initials are C.B—Charles Beagon." She backed herself into a wall and slid down it. Pulling her knees to her chest, she rocked herself.

She sat there listening to her heart hammering mixed with dripping water. Slowly, she ran her hands over the cold brick strung with cobwebs. She clutched her throat as her breath hitched in the back. She couldn't see a thing.

She clamored over the hunk of armor that fell with her, wishing a real knight would save her.

"It's just darkness. It's just darkness," she told herself. "Nothing to be afraid of. Or, as Penny would say, have a 'pancake' attack over." The thought of her silly sister brought a slight smirk to her face. She took a deep, shaky breath. "I've come this far solving this mystery; I am not going to let a little darkness stop me now. I can do this."

She felt her way to the next wall looking for a light switch. She ran her hands over rough wood shelves and cold, leaking water pipes but couldn't find what she was looking for.

After no luck, she decided to turn into a bat and use echolocation to get out.

POOF! She transformed and suspended herself in the air. She opened her mouth and made a series of popping and clicking sounds. Finally, she was able to find the chute she'd come down. But she also found something that sent a shiver through her body—someone was standing in the room with her.

POOF!

"Who's there! What do you want?" Ellie cried at the mystery person.

"To give you back your necklace," said a deep voice. The light flicked on, revealing the empty, leaky basement. There were only a few dusty shelves and a pile of broken chairs.

"Don't be alarmed," Sam said, holding up his hands. From the left, the necklace dangled. "I can explain everything." Ellie marched up to him with a burst of bravery and snatched her pendant.

Sam gave a crooked smile. "Nice to see feistiness runs in your family."

"What is that supposed to mean?" Ellie asked while analyzing her necklace.

Sam shook his head. "A story for another time." He pulled another dragon pendant out of his pocket. "That is the real one. I just needed to borrow it to make a fake. I was hoping to give it back before you even knew, but being sneaky was never my strong suit."

Ellie squinted at the man with his bushy salt-and-pepper beard and kind green eyes. Something about him seemed familiar, but she couldn't put her finger on it.

"Why would you give Henry a fake?" Ellie asked. "Aren't you worried he will take back all the artifacts that you STOLE?" She wasn't sure where her bravery was coming from. But her whole body tingled with a fiery warmth. Sam sat down on a rickety wooden chair that looked like it would crumble any second.

"I worked my whole life finding artifacts and putting them back where they belong. I've always believed that artifacts are meant to be used, especially vampire ones. They aren't meant for stuffy museums for people to gawk at."

Ellie eyed his perfectly flat teeth as he smiled. "But you aren't even a vampire," she said. "Why do you care?"

"You don't need to be something to care about it," Sam explained. "You have human friends, don't you? And you love them even though you're a vampire."

Ellie pulled the necklace back over her head, and her voice softened. "Yes. But why should I believe you about the necklace? How do I know these aren't both fake?" Sam stood up, reached into his pocket, and pulled out a photo.

"This should help. When you're ready, grab this and it will take you back upstairs," he said. "I'm afraid it will be a dark journey, but you can stop Henry. Just give me two minutes to give Henry the necklace and get out of here. Oh, and tell your friend Fez he can keep my old camera."

"Wait! You can't just leave me here!" Ellie said.

"You can leave as soon as you grab that photo," he said. His eyes went glassy. "And please, tell your grandma that Sam says hello." Before Ellie could ask how he knew her grandmother, he disappeared in a puff of white smoke.

She rushed over to the photo on the chair. Her eyes trailed over the black and white ink that showed her grandmother laughing with a man. She couldn't be more than eighteen. Her hair was dark like Ellie's, and she wore the dragon necklace around her neck. Her fangs contrasted the man's flat teeth, and she appeared to be touching a scrape on his eyebrow. Taking a deep breath, Ellie picked up the photo. Suddenly, her body rocketed through the air as if it were zooming down an invisible waterslide. Unable to move any of her limbs, she sped through the blackness. A small speck of light grew bigger with every second until it swallowed her whole.

With a sputtering sound, she landed on the hall floor beside Jessica.

"Oh, sweet pudding! We were so worried!"

Jessica said. She dove to the floor and gave Ellie the tightest hug. "Where did you go? How did you get back?" As Jessica released Ellie, she picked up the pendant. "And how did you get this back?" she asked.

"I'll explain later," Ellie said. "Where did the boys go?"

"To interrogate Clara," Jessica answered.

Ellie shook her head. "It isn't Clara. Her hands are too shaky to make initials that neat. We need to find Henry. AKA Charles Beagon. Let's go!"

Chapter 15

I Remember Everything

Ellie ran into the dining room just as Henry was giving a speech to the crowd of guests. "I want to thank you all for being here tonight. We weren't sure if we would be able to open the exhibit due to some thefts."

Gasps and whispers erupted from the crowd.

Henry adjusted his bowtie. "But don't worry, I solved the case."

"Yeah, you're the thief!" Ellie shouted.

Henry's eyes widened. "Security! This little girl has been banned from the museum for life. Please show her out." Ellie's mother stepped out of the crowd, her red dress sparkling under the chandelier's glow.

"Excuse me. You will not be kicking out my

daughter," she exclaimed.

Henry pinched the bridge of his nose. "Fine, stay. Have some food and drinks. Just, please, don't interrupt."

"Kind of hard to do when you lured me here to steal my necklace. But guess what?" Ellie pointed to it. "I got it back." Henry's face turned a sickly white as he patted his pocket. "Whatever is in your pocket is fake," Ellie added.

Henry took a sip of wine and gave an awkward laugh. "Come on, why would I want a silly trinket? Is anyone actually going to believe this little girl?"

Ellie's grandmother stepped out of the crowd. "I sure am!"

"Grandma!" Ellie cheered. She lunged toward her grandma and hugged her.

"Hi, Pudding Pop," Grandma said before kissing Ellie on the head. She turned her focus back to Henry.

"Now, I know, Henry, that you didn't just call my granddaughter a liar." She stepped toward him, her short heels clicking loudly in

the quiet room. "Surely not after chasing that necklace for the last forty years. My whole career trying to get artifacts back to their rightful families, I had you nipping at my heels. 'This belongs in a museum,' you said. 'Vampires are going to die out and don't need these things,' you said."

Shocked faces in the crowd quickly turned red with anger. They advanced toward Henry, bumping Ellie left and right. Ellie untangled from the group just as the parents of her friend Ava Grinko slipped out the front door.

"She's exaggerating," Henry said, backing away. "I think old age is getting to you and you aren't remembering correctly."

"I remember everything," she snarled. "And I'm going to add what you did to my grandbaby to the list."

Henry wiped a bead of sweat off his forehead. "Fine! Do you want me to admit that I stole the real painting and statue and broke the fake one? Because I did." The crowd paused. "Unfortunately, Ellie and her pesky friends were better detectives than I expected.

I thought 'Oh, she's just a kid, so I can get her to think it's Clara who committed the crime.' I didn't want to have to pay that old bat five years of saved vacation days when she retires. And if she were caught stealing, I wouldn't have to!"

Clara stood at the back of the room with Tink, Fez, and Carter. "You always were cheap!" she yelled. "Unless it comes to the flowers for events. Those roses cost more than you pay me in a year!"

Henry rolled his eyes. "All I wanted was to finally get that necklace *and* get rid of Clara all in one swoop. But I guess it's true what they say—you can't have it all. I should have just gotten the necklace and reported those artifacts stolen for the insurance money."

Clara shook her head. "You always did make things more complicated than they needed to be." Bright car lights blinked through the window.

"Woah! What's that?!" Henry yelled. He bolted past the distracted crowd and out the front door.

Almost every guest raced after him, but he was already hopping in a car by the time they got outside. The white SUV's tires screeched as it sped away. The flash of Fez's camera went off, leaving Ellie seeing white spots.

"Boy, if you are going to use that camera, you better figure out that flash," clucked Clara. Everyone laughed but Ellie.

"You okay?" Grandma asked.

Ellie sighed. "Yes, but I can't believe he got away."

Ellie's grandma gave her a squeeze. "Still a mystery well solved. Now, let's go home so I can tell you about your necklace."

Chapter 16
Sweet and Spicy

Ellie grabbed a tray of hot chocolate from her mother in the kitchen. The smell was sweet and comforting. And just a bit spicy thanks to a dash of red pepper.

"Are you sure you aren't sad about the art show?" Ellie asked for the tenth time.

"Stuff happens," Mrs. Spark said. "There will be other art shows. Better art shows. Plus, I missed your dad for this one. Maybe I will pick the next one for when he isn't working out of town."

Ellie grinned. "I like that idea." She brought the warm drink to her friends in the living room. Penny was already passed out, snoring on the couch, but Jessica, Tink, and Fez were all gathered around her grandmother. After the warm drinks were handed out, Ellie sat down, and her grandmother started.

"I found the necklace on one of my digs, and I knew it was special as soon as I held it." Ellie clutched where her dragon pendant usually hung on her chest, but all she got was a fistful of air. She must have slipped it off when she took off her detective coat. "It wasn't long before I figured out it could grant wishes," Grandma continued.

Fez turned to Ellie. "You're like a genie!"

Grandma laughed. "Not quite. You see, only Ellie gets to make the wish. Or whoever is wearing the necklace. She can't give the wish away. And she only gets to make a wish if the bravery meter is full."

"What's that?" Tink asked. He slurped his hot chocolate, which gave him a marshmallow mustache.

Grandma licked her thumb and cleaned his face before continuing. "You see, every time Ellie did something really brave, it would fill the meter, and she could then make a wish. It couldn't just be anything that takes courage though—it had to be a big thing. And every time she got scared, it would drain some of the wishing power."

Jessica leaned closer to the crackling fireplace. "How do you know when it's ready for a wish?"

"It glows," Grandma answered.

Fez gasped. "I saw it do that one time! Remember, at the Garlic Festival in the tent. Ellie dressed up as a clown even though she was afraid of them."

"I do remember," Tink said. "Freaky. What wish did you get, Ellie?"

Ellie shrugged. "I don't remember wishing for anything… wait! But I do remember wishing for Jack to turn purple after our jellyfish mystery!"

Grandma laughed. "You're telling me you used your wishing power to turn some boy purple?"

"I think I also wished for our first mystery when the royal wedding got frozen. AND that there were enough tickets for all of us to go to Mega Adventureland after that movie set mystery." Ellie paused, then gasped. "I just remembered, I did wish for something after the Garlic Festival. I wished to meet Hailey Haddie!"

"Those sound better than turning a boy purple," Grandma said with a fangy smile. "Now, I have to get some shut-eye."

"Wait! I have so many more questions," Ellie said. "Why didn't you tell me about how special the necklace was before? Why did you give something so powerful to me in the first place?"

Grandma dug a tattered leather journal out of her giant purse. "I think this will answer some of your questions," she said. Ellie ran her fingers over the leafy vines burnt into the cover and faded gold initials, 'L.L.' "This journal belonged to your Grandpa Leo," Grandma explained. Ellie flipped through the tatty, yellow pages packed with drawings and writing.

Grandma kissed all the kids on the forehead before scooping Penny off the sofa. "Goodnight," she whispered before carrying Penny to bed.

After discussing what Ellie would wish for now that she knew about the necklace, the mystery team headed to the front door.

"You guys are the best!" Ellie said before they left. "I'm lucky to have friends as great as you."

"We're lucky to know a detective as great as you. And I suppose you're a pretty good friend," Jessica said with a wink. "See you tomorrow!"

Ellie couldn't stop yawning as she headed to

her bedroom. As much as she wanted to read the journal, her eyes were heavy and bleary. She figured she wouldn't get past the first page before falling asleep. As she bent down to slip it under her mattress, the photo that Sam had given her fell from her pocket and fluttered to the floor. Ellie poked it before picking it up—afraid it would transport her again. She could safely say she was done with museums for a while.

Once it seemed safe, she picked up the photo and went to the attic.

Creak. Crack. Creak.

"Grandma," Ellie whispered at the top of the loud stairs. Grandma sat on the end of a cot in the middle of the art studio.

"What can I do for you?" she asked.

Ellie held up a photo. "I met a man named Sam Thomlin today, and he asked that I say hi to you. I also think you may want this." She handed the old photo to her grandma.

"My, does this bring back memories," Grandma said with tears running down her cheeks. "He was my best friend when I was just a little older than you." She sighed. "That feels like a lifetime ago now. Oh, my sweet Ellie, don't be in too much of a rush to grow up. It goes so fast." She clenched the photo to her chest.

"I won't," Ellie whispered. She cuddled beside her grandmother in the small cot. "Why have I never heard of Sam before?" she asked after a couple minutes. But the only answer she got were small snores.

As Ellie drifted to sleep, she thought about her friends and all their adventures.

Someday she would be an adult. And everyone would know to call Detective Ellie for their mysteries. She was excited for that day. But she decided she didn't want to rush it. For now, being a junior detective and even a Scaredy Bat was fine by her.

Hi!

Did you enjoy the mystery?

I know I did!

If you want to join the team as we solve more mysteries, then **leave a review**!

Otherwise, we won't know if you're up for the next mystery. And when we go to solve it, you may never get to hear about it!

You can leave a review wherever you found the book.

The gang and I are excited to see you in the next mystery adventure!

Fingers crossed there's nothing scary in that one...

Free

Minute Mystery Short Story

As a gift, we'd like to send you a FREE Minute Mystery called

"The Case of the Leaping Laboratory" so you can continue the mystery-solving fun!

GO HERE TO GET

YOUR FREE MINUTE MYSTERY NOW:

scaredybat.com/bundle2

Don't miss

Book #7 in the

Scaredy Bat

series!

Learn more at:

scaredybat.com/book6next

Are You Afraid of the Dark?

Nyctophobia [nik-tuh-foh-bee-uh] is the intense and persistent fear of night or darkness. It comes from "nyktos," the Greek word for night, and "phóbos," the Greek word for fear.

Fear Rating: Nyctophobia is one of the most

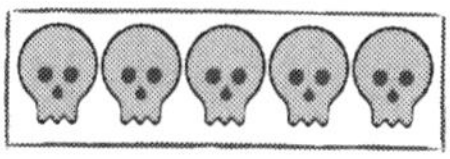

common phobias among children and to varying degrees adults. People with this phobia may experience dry mouth, dizziness, sweating, and panic attacks.

Origin: Fear of the dark may be caused by an instinctual survival response, a negative or traumatic past experience, and thoughts of hidden dangers.

Fear Facts:

- People with nyctophobia may have trouble sleeping, have panic attacks in dark places like the movies, and avoid leaving the house after dark.
- Some fear of the dark is natural, especially as a phase of child development.
- There is always some light, though humans may not be able to see it.
- Some beautiful things can only be seen in the dark, like the stars and moon.
- Tips: Set up a calm room, check for scary things, & think happy thoughts.

Jokes: Why is Dark spelled with a 'K' and not a 'C'?
Because you can't 'C' in the dark

Fear No More! With time and perspective, most can conquer the fear of darkness. But if you believe you suffer from nyctophobia and want help, talk to your parents or doctor about treatments. For more fear facts, visit: scaredybat.com/bundle2.

Suspect List

Fill in the suspects as you read, and don't worry if they're different from Ellie's suspects. When you think you've solved the mystery, fill out the "who did it" section on the next page!

Name: Write the name of your suspect

Motive: Write the reason why your suspect might have committed the crime

Access: Write the time and place you think it could have happened

How: Write the way they could have done it

Clues: Write any observations that may support the motive, access, or how

Suspect 1

Draw below

Name:
Motive:
Access:
How:
Clues:

Suspect 2

Draw below

Name:
Motive:
Access:
How:
Clues:

Suspect 3

Draw below

Name:
Motive:
Access:
How:
Clues:

Suspect 4

Draw below

Name:
Motive:
Access:
How:
Clues:

Who Did It?

Now that you've identified all of your suspects, it's time to use deductive reasoning to figure out who actually committed the crime! Remember, the suspect must have a strong desire to commit the crime (or cause the accident) and the ability to do so.

For more detective fun, visit:
scaredybat.com/bundle2

Name:
Motive:
Access:
How:
Clues:

Hidden Details Observation Sheet
-- Level One --

1. What game was Ellie playing when she was accidentally locked in the closet?
2. Who was the unknown caller on the phone?
3. What was Ellie afraid of at the beginning of the story?
4. What was the location of the mystery Ellie was asked to solve?
5. What was apparently stolen from the museum?
6. What is the troublesome Sam Thomlin?
7. What song did Fez play on the piano to open the secret door?
8. What did the kids find in the corner of the secret room?
9. What did Sam give Ellie in the basement?
10. Who was behind all the missing art and artifacts?

Hidden Details Observation Sheet
-- Level Two --

1. How did Ellie get to the museum?
2. What fell when the museum alarm went off?
3. What did Tink and Carter use to test if the marble is real?
4. What was the fake ruby made of?
5. What did Fez drop that revealed the red laser beam?
6. What familiar object did Ellie notice painted in the mural?
7. Who grabbed Ellie's necklace in the secret room?
8. What did Ellie knock over when she fell through a secret wall chute?
9. Who was the surprise guest that Ellie's mom brought to the art show?
10. What special power does Ellie's necklace have?

Hidden Details Observation Sheet
-- Level Three --

1. What does Ellie's mom use the attic for?
2. What is the name of the purple lemons on the museum tree sculpture?
3. Which museum room key supposedly went missing?
4. Who was the art curator?
5. What was the name of the black roses in the museum event room?
6. What was Clara planning to do after she retires from the museum?
7. What do the initials C.B. stand for?
8. What old fashioned device did Fez find in the secret room?
9. What kind of vehicle did Henry escape in?
10. What did Ellie's grandma give her to answer her questions about the necklace?

Answer Key

Level One Answers

1. Hide-and-seek
2. Henry Beagon
3. The dark
4. Brookside Vampire Artifact Museum
5. A painting
6. A ghost
7. Twinkle Twinkle Little Star
8. The missing painting and statue head
9. Her necklace
10. Henry Beagon

Level Two Answers

1. Bicycle
2. A sculpted marble head
3. Vinegar and a fork
4. Strawberry candy
5. A powdered donut hole
6. Her necklace
7. The ghost of Sam Thomlin
8. Knight armor
9. Grandma
10. It grants wishes

Level Three Answers

1. Art studio
2. Violem
3. Archive Room
4. Clara Burg
5. Bat Breath Roses
6. Cut hair
7. Charles Beagon
8. A camera
9. A white SUV
10. A journal that belonged to Grandpa Leo

Discussion Questions

1. What did you enjoy about this book?
2. What are some of the themes of this story?
3. How did the characters use their strengths to solve the mystery together?
4. What is your favorite museum and why?
5. Have you ever been afraid of the dark?
6. How did Ellie overcome her fear?
7. If there was a secret passage in your house, where would it be?
8. What other books, shows, or movies does this story remind you of?
9. What do you think will happen in the next book in the series?
10. If you could talk to the author, what is one question you would ask her?

For more discussion questions, visit:
scaredybat.com/bundle2

Also by Marina J. Bowman

THE LEGEND OF PINEAPPLE COVE

A fantasy-adventure series for kids with bravery, kindness, and friendship. If you like reimagined mythology and animal sidekicks, you'll love this legendary story!

thelegendofpineapplecove.com/sbb2

About the Author

Marina J. Bowman is a writer and explorer who travels the world searching for wildly fantastical stories to share with her readers. Ever since she was a child, she has been fascinated with uncovering long lost secrets and chasing the mythical, magical, and supernatural. For her current story, Marina is investigating a charming town in the northern US, where vampires and humans live in harmony.

Marina enjoys sailing, flying, and nearly all other forms of transportation. She never strays far from the ocean for long, as it brings her both inspiration and peace. She stays away from the spotlight to maintain privacy and ensure the more unpleasant secrets she uncovers don't catch up with her.

As a matter of survival, Marina nearly always communicates with the public through her representative, Devin Cowick. Ms. Cowick is an entrepreneur who shares Marina's passion for travel and creative storytelling and is the co-founder of Code Pineapple.

Marina's last name is pronounced baʊmən, and rhymes with "now then."

Made in the USA
Columbia, SC
07 September 2023

22579079R00250